A JOURNEY
WITH GOD

SO BE IT

A JOURNEY WITH GOD THROUGH
SPACE AND TIME THAT WILL IMPACT
THE FUTURE OF RELIGION AND
BELIEFS FOR THE NEXT MILLENIUM.

HARRY E. HELLER

A JOURNEY WITH GOD: SO BE IT

©Copyright 2017

TXu 2-034-049

Harry E. Heller

Print ISBN: 978-1-54391-366-8

eBook ISBN: 978-1-54391-367-5

AUTHOR'S NOTE

This book (So Be It) is a description of a journey taken by a famous character who guides a traveler to better understand the purpose of the journey.

There are three different type faces that are used for the major story:

Narrative: The narrative of the story is written in this type face.

Famous Character: "When the famous character speaks to the traveler, he uses this type face." (Always in bold quote marks -- imagine his words are spoken in a deep sonorous tone.)

Traveler: *"When the traveler communicates with the famous character and others during the journey, his comments use this format—bold italics type face surrounded by parentheses."*

All the opinions expressed by the famous character and/or the traveler are the opinions of the character. The reader is invited to accept or reject their opinions.

ACKNOWLEDGEMENTS

As a novelist, I work alone, but throughout the writingprocess, there were several people that helped me and contributed to this book. Annette Heller encouraged me to use my imagination and stretch my ideas; Dr. Lisa Roth commented on the writings and made some good suggestions; Teri Kennedy did an initial edit and sharpened some of the ideas; Andrew Roth and Molly Allanoff were the best literary experts I know, my colleagues in the Amagansett Writers Collective, run by Kara Westerman, who never discouraged but always offered new ideas.

CHAPTER
ONE

The Dreams of the Dreamer's Wife

How can I describe myself, but as a Dreamer? Only as an average guy who was chosen to help the people of the world reach perfection? I started as a creative kid. I stood up and spoke at family events, I dedicated a building when I was 10, I lead discussions, told jokes, and debated political points while I whizzed through high school with average grades because I was bored. Since my wife, Annie, is an important contributor to this story, I'll tell you about her as well. We met at a party given to enable young boys and girls who were Jewish to meet. She was 14 and I was 17. I was ready to get into City College of New York – a free public college. She was in Rapid Advance.

My parent's only concern was that I should stay close to our religious beliefs. They were sure that away from home I would become an Agnostic. I promised them I wouldn't but when my literature professor taught us that the Bible was written by men, it was a shock to me. I always thought that God, Him or Herself, wrote the

Bible. So, I am not an agnostic, but after the trip I took in my adventure, I now have a different perception of the role of a Supreme Being.

When Annie became college age, she and I shared CCNY as a school. I was an engineering student and after graduating worked several years designing weapons systems for the U.S. Air Force. I quit my job and after four years of night school, I received a Ph.D. in Social Psychology. Then, I became an advertising man and later the president of a company doing public opinion surveys. Annie took a degree in education (a teacher) and after graduating, became a school psychologist. After that, she worked as an entrepreneur, crafting and selling jewelry to Bloomingdales and Bergdorf-Goodman. Years later, she owned a facility to do marketing research interviews. Not long after first meeting, we fell in love. Since we came from families where marriage was forever, we wooed each other and married at 20 and 23 years of age.

Both of us earned more than our parents could ever imagine. When we had two children – Lara and Dave – the four of us travelled, lived in a house in a Long Island suburb, owned an apartment in Greenwich Village and a vacation home in East Hampton. We also lived a spiritual life, frequently praying at a synagogue and talking about the meaning of life, what follows life, and how we will deal with it when it approaches. Almost every morning, Annie told me her dreams, often filled with appearances by her dead parents, uncles and aunts (some of whom Annie had never met because they did not survive the Holocaust).

Annie channeled her spiritual experiences by becoming an abstract artist and developed techniques of representing profound religious and spiritual concepts using this creative talent. We studied the Kabbalah together, a mystical book, and the two of us explored sacred texts of the spiritual aspects of religion. She did 10 paintings of the "Emanations" of the Kabbalah. The eight bridges linking the process of creating and perfecting. These eight bridges included two aspects of Knowledge (Right Brain or Left Brain), two aspects of Judgement (Merciful or Punishing), two aspects of Outcomes (Personal Success or Beating a Foe), and two aspects of Aesthetics (Beauty or Solidity). Many of these insights were developed with my help as my late maternal grandfather was a well-known Talmudist. It was clear with my abilities to interpret, orate, debate, and lead discussions in the family, I must have inherited some of his genes.

When we woke up every morning, we compared dreams, sharing our time together. But all good things must end, and Annie contracted breast cancer at the age of 50. From the time it was first diagnosed, she lived another 25 years. Those years were filled with travel, art, and family milestones as our two children began their own families. Annie was a doting, patient grandmother who spent a lot of time with the grandchildren; playing ball with the three boys and teaching the two granddaughters her abstract painting techniques, which included ways of mixing colors and laying down a base color on a canvas.

Annie fought her cancer through chemotherapy. In the beginning, the side effects were tolerable. But Annie, a beauty all her life, lost her blond curly hair, the brightness of her face, and the athleticism that enabled her to raise funds by running marathons and 10K's for leukemia, breast cancer, and a local hospital. About six months before her passing, she decided to stop chemo because the side effects became worse than the disease. Still, one month before her death, the entire family shared a vacation on the beach on St. Barths, her favorite Caribbean Island. I carried out the usual duties for the family. First thing in the morning, I walked down the beach to a bakery, purchased croissants, and made some dark coffee in our room to share at breakfast. When we left our oceanfront apartment, we spent several hours on the soft white sand and went for a dip in the azure blue waters. In the afternoon, we dressed and drove down into town to visit *Stephane and Bernard*, a shop where she purchased French designer clothes, duty-free. She was aware that this would be the last time she would be there, but we had a daughter, daughter-in-law and two lovely granddaughters, and we were buying the clothes for them, not for her. At night, I recreated our "salad days" as all of us went to a Michelin 3-star restaurant for a great French meal washed down with a bottle of Bordeaux wine. These were great memories. In Annie's last days, our family celebrated our 57th anniversary and a family Passover Seder. She died quietly on the last day of Passover, surrounded by the family.

In our many private discussions, Annie had promised that she would try to reach me after she died. I told her I wasn't sure if she would be able to do it. She reminded me that Moses received advice from a talking Burning Bush, the Prophets often communed with God, Jonah and Jacob argued and fought with God, Jesus spoke to God as his Father, and the famous Rabbis were often in dream states in prayer. Annie's recommendation was that I should look for her in my dreams after she was gone.

When Annie died, the family, both children and adults, went back to their lives, jobs, and schools, and used her foibles as wonderful memories and loving experiences.

On the other hand, I lived alone in our beach house, inviting family and guests to visit, but every night sleeping alone in our bed. When I slept, my dreams were filled with her presence.

My dreams were also filled with the Sacred Texts we had worked on when Annie was painting; their meaning, their impact, and their way of guiding us in paths of truth, kindness and life. My dreams went on, with or without her, but sometimes within me.

One night Annie came into my dream in a lucid way. She was happy with how the family and I were flourishing. She suddenly communicated to me that there was an important apparition with whom she had spoken, my maternal grandfather Morris, the famous Talmudic scholar. He told her, "He was following me and pleased that I had succeeded in being a kind and moral person." He said, "As much as he was able to understand the Commandments in the Talmud when he was alive, he never really knew if his interpretations were right until he had reached the afterlife." He had been in the presence of one of the highest spirits in the afterlife who told him that "he had inspired a series of scrolls on The Holy Land that had not been found, and unless they were found, the meaning of life and God could never be fully understood on Earth." My grandfather suggested that "If my grandson can find them and interpret them, he can change the world."

Annie asked him, "How can he find these scrolls?"

He told her, "They are at N32.0518103 and E35.2868358." Annie read these numbers to me quickly as I went into REM sleep.

I had to remember these strings of letters and numbers, but I couldn't wake up recalling them all. I believed I had the first four numbers: N32.05 and E35.28.

After I wrote down those numbers, I entered them into Google to see what they meant. The N represented a Latitude, measured from the Equator 32.05 degrees north; the E represented a Longitude 35.28 degrees east of the Greenwich Mean Time Line. Where these two lines meet is where the Scrolls would be found. Again, I put these two lines into Google and they intersected in Shiloh, Israel. When I read about Shiloh, I discovered it was a city of ancient Canaan. I was amazed to learn that archeologists have been finding major scrolls in Shiloh for over thousands of years. Why did my Grandpa Morris give me the responsibility to change the world? I'm a Senior Citizen, not the child he played with when I was three years old.

Now, what do I do? To find the scrolls I would need the final four digits that I failed to remember. I would have to go to sleep, hoping that Annie could remember them. Who knows if her afterlife memory is an issue? I would dream, get the numbers, write them down, and hope I could recall them. I was given the numbers initially, why didn't I just write them down then? However, if I had seen the numbers, perhaps they were stored in my memory? I must have had some associative memory that I may have used. I sat down on a couch and set up a CD of Pachelbel's Canon trying to picture the last four numbers of each that I may have seen. I forced out the first memory – my childhood Brooklyn address – 2103. I was only sure of the 103. Maybe 2103, 3103, 4103, 5103, 6103, 7103, 8103 – BINGO, that was it. Now go for the other numbers. My age, 82, and my last anniversary, 57, both plus one: 83 and 58. So the four numbers missing were 8103 and 8358. I jumped up like a child and screamed, hoping that my neighbor would not call the police.

The next morning, I called El Al Airlines for a reservation, pulled my luggage out of the closet, and contacted Shmuel, my nephew in Israel to ask him to find a geographer who understood geographic positioning. I had been to Israel several times and it is a long trip on an often crowded plane. I have found that at my age, I must reserve in first/business class. There, the El Al cabin provides a seat that turns into a bed. Plus, the check-in procedure puts you on an express line.

But the airline still provides well-trained screeners to find potential terrorists. When I wheeled my bag to the check-in counter, a young man casually walked over to me and asked, "May I see your passport?" I showed it to him. "Why are you going to Israel?"

(I can't tell him that my dead grandfather wants me to save the world!) "I'm visiting my nephew and studying ancient texts in Shiloh."

"What does your nephew do for a living?"

"He is retired and visits his children and grandchildren."

"Who does he visit?"

"Well, I know his son is in a tank brigade in northern Israel, and his son-in-law used to be an aide to the former Prime Minister."

"Where does the former aide live?"

"Jerusalem." I replied.

"Have you ever been to Israel?"

My answer was a brag. "I have been there many times, the first time before you were born, in 1952."

He smiled, handed me my passport, and said, "Have a good time with your nephew."

On the plane, I watched the first 10 minutes of a movie and decided I needed sleep, not Jennifer Aniston. I set the seat on horizontal with my feet elevated and told the flight attendant that I didn't want dinner, but to wake me for breakfast. My Yoga teacher had told me that the best way to rest is with your feet higher than your heart. Quickly, I went to sleep to the whir of the Rolls Royce engines.

The sleep was fitful, but I dreamed and Annie managed to enter my consciousness. She said, "Your grandfather was told by his heavenly colleague that if you find the scrolls, you should handle them carefully, put them in a small closed tent, and set it up exactly 1,000 meters north of the mosaic floor of the ancient synagogue in Shiloh. He will appear to you in the tent as a dream.

After I landed in Israel, my nephew, Shmuel picked me up at the airport in Israel. He took me to his house in Ra'anana, a lovely town settled by Modern Orthodox arrivals, many English speaking. Near this town is Herzlyia, a seacoast town with 5-star hotels. I offered to buy them dinner at a new kosher restaurant in town and Shmuel invited Marty Slivovitz, an American living near him, to join us. I found it hard not to make fun of his name, it being the same as a brand of plum brandy consumed on Holidays. Marty was an expert in town planning, which provided the skills of GPS location, and he appeared to be a classic nerd. He also had an App in his iPhone that measured longitudes and latitudes to double check his physical measurements. We had a dinner of pita and hummus, salad, lamb chops, and a bottle of red wine. Shmuel suggested I choose a wine from Shiloh. The wine was great, considering that the vines were 2,000 years old.

Shmuel suggested that I stay overnight with him, but I had already reserved a room at the Ritz Carlton in Herzlyia, overlooking the Mediterranean Sea. It had a plunge bath, gym, and a 4-star chef. (As with the El Al decision, I like my comfort.) We decided to start out at 8AM to go to Shiloh.

Waking up at 7AM is like waking up at midnight in New York. But I had a fitful sleep, aided by an Excedrin PM. Anxious as I was, I woke up at 6AM. I took a hot plunge bath and had an Israeli breakfast with pancakes, different fish and bagels washed down with three cups of espresso. Shmuel and Marty picked me up on time and we drove north on the Tel Aviv – Haifa Road. After about 45 minutes, we turned onto a highway heading due east into what the Arabs call the West Bank and the Jews call Judea and Samaria. It reminded me that two sets of people have different histories. On our way, we stopped at a camping store and I purchased a tent with a 10x10 foot floor, a hammer and a chisel, a flashlight, and a bunch of protein bars. I didn't know who I would be meeting, but it is unlikely that he would not need snacks – as I would. We barely got the tent into the car trunk. By their furtive looks from Shmuel and Marty, it was apparent that they knew I was looking for something and I could not tell them. As we entered the Shiloh area they passed an Israeli checkpoint who reviewed the safest routes and examined the bulging trunk. I told them I would be meeting someone in the tent and if I needed a lift back, I would call Shmuel.

When we reached Shiloh, it took five hours of Marty giving Shmuel directions. "A wall…let's go around the wall…up that street, slight right, etc." Finally, we got out and followed Marty on foot. He came very close to the target intersection. It was an empty house, barely standing, practically falling apart, probably from the 8 to 10 wars fought there against the Romans, Greeks, Assyrians, the 1948 War of Israel Independence, and perhaps the Hezbollah shelling from Lebanon in the 1980's. However, it did appear to have a basement under the rubble. We walked around with the flashlight. Marty asked me, "Hey do you have an archeological permit?"

I told him, "Marty, I don't need a permit because I am looking for something a friend lost here." (Wow, what a lie!) Using the hammer and chisel, I tapped around the floor, the walls, the ceiling, and any area that something I didn't know about could be. Was this a fool's task? I thought. I compared the sound of each tap to the previous tap. No luck until one tap had a double sound like wood and marble: "Crash-ping." This must be it, whatever "it" is.

I told Shmuel and Marty to go to the car, open the trunk, and wait for me. I chipped away at the space of the sound, then around it. As more of the wall crumbled, I could free the wood cover. Some of the wood rotted away as I pulled on it and I saw a marble undercover. I chiseled away around the space and pulled the box out, part rotted wood, part a marble box, virtually airtight. The marble box was 15" by 12" and 9" high. It was not heavy so I carefully ran out with it and put it in the trunk of the car, covering it with my grandson's Penn State windbreaker. I jumped into the car and I asked my nephew if he knew where the mosaic floor of the synagogue was. "Of course I do, we come here all the time with the family during the holidays." He drove to it and arrived just before the sun was setting.

I asked Marty, "Can you identify a spot 1,000 meters due north of the center of the mosaic floor?" Marty made a few calculations and paced off toward the north. The iPhone App had enabled him to get an exact location. Shmuel drove the car to the spot and we pitched the tent right there. I put the marble box in the middle of the tent, still covered with my grandson's windbreaker. My nephew suggested to me that this spot is in the middle of a Greek *Temenos* (a wooden structure), like the way the ark of the covenant was placed in a tent.

We spoke about this exciting day. Shmuel and Marty asked me, "Do you really want to take this risk?" So I ask them, "What's the risk?" Marty pointed across a valley and said, "You see those lights about a half a mile up the hill, it is an Arab village, probably nice guys so stay close to the tent." I thanked them for their help and told Shmuel that I would be in touch with him as soon as I could. But he should not worry for I was being protected in a way that I could not share with him right then. When the time was right, I would let him know what I was doing.

About 10 minutes after they left, at sundown, there was a bright light illuminating the tent. An apparition came inside and spoke to me in a deep sonorous voice, **"I will read to you the beginning of the scrolls I left here 2500 years ago."** He was short but he had a muscular legs and strong arms. He had a white beard around his chin but surprisingly he had short furry hair on his arms and legs. Then he removed the cover of the marble box. It was filled with a neat stack of flat parchments. I spoke back, thinking ahead about my potential future interactions with him. I asked him, **"What happens** *if I have a question for you about something I did not understand?"* Using a thick pen so I could write in dark ink, I penned a sentence on the top of a sheet of paper in English, assuming he would understand it.

"If you want to ask me something or want me to clarify anything based upon my experiences, I will communicate like this to your narrative and share my knowledge and experience.

He replied to me, "**I will understand and respect your insights as I shared those of your grandfather.**

He picked up the first parchment, floated it to his guest, and in a loud and booming voice that shook the tent he declared, "**I begin:**"

The First Paragraph: Hail to Planet SS396-P3 (Solar System 396 Planet 3 from the sun): "My name is *Ya-Ha-Va-Ha*. I am the leader the planet of *Shamym*, which has sent out 362 emissary fleets under my overall command. These fleets have gone to many areas of the universe. My expedition party from Shamym has visited your planet, we call it **Aretz**, and left signs and symbols on it. We hope you will find the right scholars in the future. If not - "**So be it**."

"My Breath was taken away when I heard who you are and my brain transferred its blood flow, making me dizzy." I continued," *Among the spiritual leaders of Aretz, [we call it "Earth"] your name is used to describe the supreme being; Ya-Ha-Va-Ha, also named El Shadai, Adonai, Allah, Yahaweh, Jehovah, Yud-heh-vav-heh, and your planet Shamym is translated to us as Heaven. Since your name is spoken rarely and quietly, may I refer to you as El Shadai? "*

He replied, "**I have used that name for Abraham, Moses, Jonah and Isaiah, so you may use it since you are the first person** in many eons to talk to me and see my continence since. I want you to know that I am not an Omnipotent God. For some reasons during my first visits to give these scrolls most of the peoples with which I interacted believed that I controlled every aspect of their life. You will see that El Shadai has many things to do to perfect the universe, rather than being angry if they fail to pray to me."

The Second Paragraph: We have chosen specific people on your planet as our converts and emissaries to accept our teachings and experiences. We hope they will be able to hand these down to others on your planet to be accepted in a peaceful way. We hope those they teach will adopt our rules. If they ignore these teachings, modify, or compromise them for their own interests, and they fail - **So be it.**

I suggested to him, *"I don't know who these converts and emissaries are but I believe they are my people that you have chosen."*

The Third Paragraph. We left this record of our visit, knowing it will be found when your people have reached the level of understanding of its meaning for you. It is written in a language that uses binary numbers representing symbols and images that you will be able to translate into a convenient linguistic system of your choice. We have no knowledge if, when, and how this will be found and translated. As the first person that has found it, you have been given a task to bring it to your civilization. If you fail in this test - **So be it**.

I answered him, *"I hope that I will be able to reach the level of understanding and I will carry the meaning to others."*

The Fourth Paragraph: In this story, we have provided a history of our planet, Shamym, and our solar system from its beginnings to the point where we have left your planet and returned home. We have revisited your planet, **Aretz,** several times and observed your "humans" (which we call, Prime-Organisms) close-up to explore what learning you have made from our experiences. Your humans may have seen us in the past. You will understand why we visited your planet if you read this. If you do not read and understand it, the impact we have made, if any, will be ingrained in you without your understanding of why we did it - **So be it.**

"I look forward to your history although I do not understand how and why your planet chose our planet.'

He answered, **"You are impatient, young man. The documents and scrolls I am leaving here tell you the entire history that has led to these emissary fleets, and to inform you as to why these fleets undertook these trips to the 362 solar systems."**

He picked up the next parchment, and in is deep voice announced, **"The History begins."**

CHAPTER
TWO

History of Shamym and the Creation of the Entire Universe

Our planet is called **Shamym.** El Shadai was selected as the leader of this planet. Shamym is one of millions of planets in many solar systems in our galaxy. Our galaxy, called "Bright Stars," is one of 170 billion galaxies in the universe. Your galaxy, which you call the "Milky Way," is one of those 170 billion galaxies.

I asked a simple question, *"I imagine you must have been listening to our transmissions or observing us?"*

But your galaxy is a great distance from ours—far from the center of the Universe,

"So it is likely that your visit to our planet was the first time you interacted with Aretz."

His answer was, **"True."**

In many inhabitable planets, we have visited, we always found and identified a high order of life we called "Prime-Organisms."

They join us on their planets and celebrate the origins of the universe and, by the physical cause and effect, the creation of Shamym, our solar system, and all the galaxies, solar systems, and the universe with which we have communicated. All of us celebrate the anniversary. The holiday is called **SHNA.**

This holiday starts and is measured at the point it takes for Shamym to reach the apogee of its oval orbit that comes closest to the center of its solar system. SHNA celebrates the beginning of the universe.

I told him about our planet, "*My people on Aretz call our planet, Earth, in many languages. One of the languages, Hebrew, calls it Aretz, so it is possible you have visited Earth. My group of people has a holiday called "Rosh Ha-Shana" [Shana- SHNA?] to celebrate the beginning of the creation of "Aretz." However, it was never possible to join with other planets or other sects on Aretz. It is likely that the Children of Israel is the group of converts you mentioned when we first met.*"

The history continued: for the duration of our holiday, and as a sign of happiness and renewal, we dress our bodies in a white cover made from a rare cloth harvested from the silica strands that were formed when intense heat melted the surface of each planet. This is found on the surface of the median diameter of Shamym.

I described our holiday, "*People of Aretz too, dress in white cloth made from materials and fur harvested from the skin of lower forms of life or plants. White is a symbol of purity and holiness.*"

The narration continued: the beginning of our universe and solar system occurred at the same time as the beginning of your solar system. We (and you) are part of a giant universe created in one explosion that led to many galaxies. Our solar system is one of many that are "close-in" within which there are planets and suns in proximity to each other. Thus, communication and trade are common within the close-in planets of the mother stars. Shamym, our planet, is the richest and most advanced planet in our solar system. It provides work and sustenance to every other planet in the solar system for one reason: we have large stores of gold. The reason why this has given us vast influence will be described later. Because Shamym controls the gold, all the decisions come from me.

Under my supervision, our scientists have discovered and written a history of the origins of our universe. We know that approximately five and one-half billion orbit apogees of Shamym have passed since the creation. The time between orbit apogees represents one year on our planet. Our orbit is an oval path around our mother star, which provides us with both light and warmth.

Our orbit is like the orbit of your planet around your mother star, which divides into 27 periods around our mother star. Your planet takes 12 periods. *"I thought, 12 Months?"* In addition to the orbit, like your planet, Shamym was set in motion to rotate around its own axis in its cooling stage.

The period of the axis rotation during which we face our mother star and experience light and warmth is called *O'hr* (like your *Day Time*) and the period during which we face away from the star is called *Choshech* (like your *Night Time*). The complete revolution encompasses O'hr and Choshech is called *Y'um* (like your *Day*). Our Y'um is 1.57 times longer than that of your planet.

21

I was curious, *"El Shadai, in the beginning of our Holy Book, there are explanations of how the Supreme Being created light and dark and combined them to day. Is this creation the one that you inspired the authors of the Holy Book to describe its creation?"*

He replied, **"Yes, I did inspire them, but they did not see me."**

The narration continues: Why do we celebrate the day of creation and what makes it a prime holiday?

The Creation of the planets in our close-in solar system (and the entire universe) celebrates a unique occurrence that started with a single bundle of energy. We estimate that it was the size of one-third of our orbit now. This bundle was solid, there was no matter outside of it. It was like a dot of energy in the middle of a dark and empty universe.

I interjected, *"You seem to be describing what our scientists call the "Big Bang." He shrugged his broad shoulders and blinked his hairy eyes not understanding "The Big Bang."*

The Narration: for some reason, all this energy was involved in a great explosion that started the expansion of the universe. Our scientists surmise that what existed prior to this event, and to this day, is a matter of pure speculation. Some of our thinkers believe it might have been triggered by a random collision of two charged particles that set off a series of collisions. Others posit that it was caused by a cosmic force beyond our powers to measure or understand. Some believe our universe might be part of an even greater universe and is merely a tiny bit of matter in this greater universe. But this is an unproven conjecture. Others believe that the force might be a power that started this process for a purpose of its own. We have never found this power.

I told him, *"The scientists of our planet (Aretz) accept the Big Bang, but many who oversee the spiritual needs of our planet do not universally accept the theory because they seek to find a way of understanding who the "being" was that started it."*

Narration: Whatever the process was, it was not a conventional explosion, but rather an event filling all of space with all the particles of the embryonic universe rushing away at great speeds from both the center and each other. They are still rushing on their way to infinity. Some of our scientists have considered that it is possible at some point for these components of the universe to lose their original energy and stop expanding. If so, the particles of the galaxies and solar systems will begin contracting as they are drawn back to an attractive force in the center. If this theory is correct, the end of the contraction will cause the end of the universe. Every planet and all living things will be destroyed in this ending. If it happens - **So be it**.

Like any random explosion, some elements of the universe that were created became non-random. Some star groupings settled close to each other. Our galaxy and solar system are an example of this. We have found and visited each of the 12 planets in our solar system. We have also visited 130 planets in 22 star groups that support intelligent life within our part of the close-in galaxy. All solar systems are made up of a mother star surrounded by planets orbiting around her and held in by gravity. Prime organisms from many of these planets have been identified. Our well-developed technology and massive strength has allowed our leader, the prophet **El Shadai**, to bring these various planets together. Some of them are in frequent communication with El Shadai.

I asked him, *"Aretz appears to be an outlier which is why we have never found life from another planet. But now it is apparent that when you wrote the scrolls and put it on our planet, you may have interacted with our humans. His answer surprised me!)* He said, **"True, you will see."**

The Narration: our scientists theorize that in the beginning, the universe was initially so hot and dense, that even elementary particles containing positive and neutral charges could not exist. Instead, different types of matter (called matter and antimatter) collided together, creating pure energy. But as the universe began to cool during the first few minutes, both positive and neutral particles began to form.

Slowly over time, these positive, neutral, and negative particles came together to form different gasses. We even found that a single elementary particle of light energy, traveling through the universe at high speeds after the initial explosion of creation, could gather other particles. This caused the elementary light particles to develop mass and become solid particles.

I mused with him, **"Only recently, the scientists of Aretz have identified this particle and we call it the Hobbs Particle."**

It was during the five billion of our orbits that followed, that stars, planets, and galaxies formed to create the universe. Five hundred million of our orbits ago, when the planet had cooled, its surface developed into solid and liquid forms, dispersing randomly. The solids were made up of minerals of various forms. The liquid was made from a combination of our most plentiful gasses – in your terminology, hydrogen and oxygen. We have found that in other planets in our close-in universe that we have reached, similar developments have occurred – a mineral surface with bi-hydrous oxide liquid in large amounts. Another element we have in plentiful amounts of is carbon – probably a by-product of the formation period of our planet and the heat emitted by our Mother star.

How Life Forms Were Created

The organisms on our planet didn't begin to exist until the most recent 250 million apogees occurred. Over the past 25 million orbits, more complex organisms developed an adequate intelligence that can enumerate the age since creation. The most advanced and sophisticated organisms are referred to as **Prime- Organisms,** which we also refer to as **Primes.**

I clarified our terminology, *"On Aretz, what you call Prime-Organisms, we call Humans."*

Narration: our scientists have found that tiny organisms developed in the liquid pools and, by a process we call *"The Strong Win Over the Weak,"* (**SWOW**), the strongest organisms survived and flourished because they found a way of adapting best to the planet. This development continued for 300 Million orbits.

When I heard the concept of SWOW, I was quick to tell El Shadai, *"This confirms Darwinism as a "universal" theory, but I imagine that many of our people will continue to deny it. Charles Darwin was an "eco-biologist" who observed and classified organisms and noticed that many of them who survived had characteristics that enabled adaptation to their surroundings."*

Narration: about 100 Million orbits ago, our SWOW system accelerated to more complex life sources. Our contact with nearby civilizations has confirmed that the basic method used for growth of all advanced organisms have much in common. Here are our observations and theories.

All organisms, including primes, develop nearly symmetrical forms or torsos. Those that survived from the SWOW principle developed a means of propulsion to move about the planet [On your planet, **Aretz**, the function of your legs and feet are developed to propel your primes in this way.] Those that emerged from SWOW also develop a means of manipulation of the environment that is also symmetrical [On your planet your arms and hands with opposing thumbs are used to maximize manipulation of objects.] The third factor that superior organisms develop because of SWOW is a thinking system with input from sensing organs [On your planet the thinking unit, eyes, ears, and touch serves these needs.]

"Our "thinking system" is called the Brain, which is used for thought and knowledge but also controlling instinctive bodily functions."

To feed these functions and interconnect them are systems of liquid carrying nourishment and a system of communication using impulses to enable them to interact.

Speaking to El Shadai, I interjected, *"Many years ago, there were scientists on Aretz that believed other life forms were based on sand and glass. However, the way in which you describe yours, and its similarity to Earth's, makes me think that life forms are truly "universal." Probably all planets were formed the same way in the Big Bang and when you have hydrogen, oxygen, nitrogen, and carbon from the cooling down, you have a life form like all the others."*

Narration: We have found in our prior contact with other beings that from this method of development, there are many different prime organisms that resulted. These are different for different planets and are often unique for various environments on any one planet.

As an example, our planet is 20,000 miles in diameter (32,187 km.) and has almost four times the gravitational pull of your planet, Aretz. Because of SWOW, organs of the body that are used to propel the weight of the torso had to be sized appropriately for the organism to acquire food and sustenance, and to escape predators. Those that survived had a muscular type of body. [So on your planet, the size of your legs and arms are smaller and weaker than ours.]

"El Shadai, I did not understand why your body had a muscular structure in your body and hand and feet. Now I know, but why do you have fur on your skin."

He read to me the next narration: Our planet was further from the sun than others were from theirs. Those of us that survived had skin layers covering our endoskeleton that were lighter in color and developed a thick layer of body fat (and in some cases hair and fur) that enabled us to survive in colder temperatures.

Because of the size of our planet, the gaseous surface stabilized into a mix of three gasses: 50% oxygen, 30% nitrogen, and 20% carbon dioxide. The lungs of organisms that survived were larger than those that failed to live because they were better able to utilize the volume of oxygen to support bodily functions.

Our planet has many organisms, and within each type the SWOW principle applies. Our prime organism is the strongest (of which I am one), mainly because we could gain control of the other organisms and use them for sustenance, although some of them are used for companionship.

We sustain ourselves by feeding on other organisms on the planet that we can control. In the 100 million orbits in which we have developed, the greatest leap we took was when we discovered that fats, proteins, and amino acids could sustain our bodies and grow our thinking processes.

"In recent studies on Earth, doctors who specialize on diet studies have accepted the importance of proteins and amino acids in the diet. Some of them have suggested that the growth of our brains may have influenced the role of human's impact as the "Alpha- Specie," our term for "prime organism."

Narration: as our solar system organisms matured through the SWOW process, we became more aware of the physical, biological, and organizations of the civilizations of our universe. We started communicating, then visiting, then working and interacting with other primes. Within the last 500 orbits, we were able to contact other planets in our universe and travelled between them, learning more about the commonality of our prime-organisms and theirs.

Life forms of other prime-organisms in our universe of planets do not substantially differ from ours. Because of the SWOW process, some have smaller propelling organs and manipulative organs. Many have larger organs of these types. Within those planets that have higher levels of oxygen, the SWOW process has resulted in smaller lung size. On a planet that has only small amounts of oxygen in the planet, SWOW has resulted in organisms that have evolved multiple lung chambers that enable them to inhale three times the amount of oxygen found on our planet.

Interplanetary travel required the development of major adjustments to the equipment used when we visit a new planet. We have developed oxygen multipliers and propulsion manipulative aids to do this.

In the beginning of our mutual development, all the planets in our close-in universe with intelligent civilizations interacted well with each other, and there were visits and treaties between various planets. Our universe uses the mineral gold as a propulsion fuel and Shamym has huge stores of gold. When planets have smaller supplies of gold, Shamym supplies the universe with most of the energy and propulsion systems. It has given us great power over other planets that use gold. Thus, the population of Shamym was among the leading technological civilizations. Our galaxy was an excellent environment in which to live and interact. Then things changed.

Since the discovery of black holes, wormholes, and warp travel, we were eventually able to reach many universes. We were not optimistic about what we would find in these galaxies. Some were so far from other stars and we felt they would never learn to be able to travel to us. But for reasons that will become clear in this narrative, we decided to monitor and make contacts with many planets in these galaxies.

We can identify and have named thousands of other star groupings. We even saw two galaxies on the very edge of our universe – one shaped like a spiral and another, the one that Aretz is in, is like a whirlpool.

Our proximity to other life forms similar to ours within our reach has accelerated our scientific knowledge. But it has also caused to identify planets on which many prime-organisms have died due to factors beyond their awareness. I will describe these factors in a later stage of this history.

CHAPTER

THREE

Life forms of The Close-in Solar System of Shamym

Our scientists have discovered that the inhabitants of different planets can be different in size, endoskeleton, body covering, and body shape. These attributes are the result of the environment of each planet and the specific process of the SWOW principle. Many other characteristics are influenced by the way our organisms respond to these differences.

Since all the planets in our close-in universe are based on a hydrocarbon environment interacting with oxygen and other specific minerals, we discovered that many of the tiny units that make up our totality are programmed during our development to complete an essential function. These we call "cells." Thus, two tiny cell organisms that start out being identical will end up being different to do an essential function. For example, one may develop the ability to absorb and process oxygen while another may become one of the millions of units that make up our fat protection to deal with our colder planetary temperature.

*I pointed out that, "**the biologists on our planet, Aretz, have also discovered cells, and there are cells in the origin of the species that can grow to unique properties for the need of a specific function. Our biologist calls them "Stem Cells."***

Our scientists have found that all the tiny cell organisms that make up our Prime-Organisms attach themselves to a grouping of cells with specific function on a spiral band. Each differentiated cell controls a unique property in the prime- organism. Fifteen hundred orbits ago, our scientists could decode this spiral band and used this knowledge to treat inherent weaknesses and defects in the prime organism.

*"**The scientists on our planet that discovered the spiral band were awarded the Nobel Prize in their science. The founder of this worldwide prize, Nobel, invented an explosive that killed many people and to atone for this invention, used his efforts to recognize scientific discovery. Our species, which I have referred to as "Humans," recognize the role of atonement in their lives. This is especially true among my tribe."***

On our planet, Shamym, our prime-organisms are classified as two different types of beings. They are referred to as *Providers* and *Birthers*. The providers contribute half of the makeup of a new prime organism and the birthers contribute the other half and allow the new prime organism to develop in the birther bodies. Many lesser organisms on our planet reproduce without a two-organism contribution, but the most advanced family of organisms, the prime-organism, use providers/birthers combination. Our scientists believe that the providers/birthers approach emerged as part of our SWOW process.

It appears that with two contributors to a prime-organism, the results are more likely to pass on characteristics that are better able to develop with fewer malformations. There are few differences between the roles of providers and birthers, and they both contribute equally to the tasks of our society. Birthers are identifiable by a symbol between their eyes when they are born, which indicates that they are able to develop an organism in the birth sac in their body. On Shamym, providers and birthers are not allowed to have more than one organism through multiple pairings, so typically each will pair with two or three other partners per the population and food needs of their group.

"The Humans of Aretz have a similar way of reproduction. What you call "Providers," we call "Males," and what you call "Birthers," we call "Females."

The transfer of the organisms between providers and birthers are by prolonged contact between the outer organ used to ingest food and communicate – the two most important tasks of our prime-organism. The provider contributes the birth organisms based upon the cells he has and the birther ingests it. The reproductive organism goes to the sac that contains the birthers' organisms based upon the birthers' cells and the two are combined in the sac. The completed prime-organism is fully developed in 1/75th part of an orbit around the sun.

I described our process to El Shadai, **"We have somewhat different ways of combining the contributions of the Males. He provides what we call "Sperm," and the Female's contribution is called an "Egg." It takes nine months to develop, or 75% of the time for a full orbit around our sun."**

On Shamym the prime-organism is raised and educated by a group specialized in doing these tasks called the **EEMAS**. When the prime organism reaches the point at which their education is complete and they reach maturity, they are assigned to a work function in the society for which they have the greatest aptitude.

I filled in our approach to child care, *"In many of our groups we have a care-giving function so that the new human (baby) learns how to live and move by itself. Surprisingly, some groups on Earth use the word EEMA to describe the caregiver, others call it OOMA. Perhaps the name of the caregiver is a "universal" way of describing this function. Or perhaps the way the baby provides sounds to call the caregiver."*

Other planets in our close-in universe have different reproduction systems, which were evolved during their SWOW development. For some, the providers and birthers have an ongoing relationship beyond reproducing. For others, the process of transfer between the providers and birthers are related to a pleasurable experience. Our scientists believe that the pleasurable experience was an outgrowth of the SWOW impact on this reproduction system. Their theory is that a pleasurable experience won out in the development of reproduction by encouraging proliferation of the prime organism. For those planets that have ongoing relationships, or are done through pleasurable experiences, the providers and birthers take greater responsibility in the education and maturity of their offspring. They also have greater bonding to their partners.

I told El Shadai, that our experience is, *"The Aretz Humans usually have ongoing relationships beyond reproduction, and the transfer between male and female is pleasurable. However, some relationships are sudden and unplanned because one or both of the partners want to experience the pleasurable task. The result of the birth in this way will often impact the life of the human baby and its training."*

Because of the method of reproduction on Shamym, our population has survived without aggression, jealousy, or strife. Indeed, even these three processes were unknown to us until we contacted the planets on our close-in universe. There, we observed their processes to variable degrees and realized it was something which we never had thought about.

"In Aretz, we appear to try to strike a balance between preventing aggression, jealousy, and strife, and in preventing the freedom to choose alternatives."

When El Shadai ruled, he ignored these observations and helped many of the planets in our solar system advance in knowledge. We supplied them with the gold used for fuel and propulsion. But we also asked my scientists to explore the spiral of organisms (that they found contained information for new organisms) to determine how aggression, jealousy, and strife are impacted by our heredity.

"We also infer from the genes in the spiral bands the capabilities for specific work and tasks."

The experiments carried out by our scientists discerned factors associated with our thinking unit – a complex organ that governs both the physical movements of our body (both voluntary or instinctual) and the logical movements. They found bodily chemicals that can change responses to certain stimuli. These chemicals differ in volume for providers and birthers as well as other Prime-Organisms with which we interact on mutually beneficial tasks that impact the absorption of some of these chemicals. These chemicals produce responses if the thinking unit believes that other prime-organisms are threatening their survival chances.

But while these chemicals pass through the organisms that define us, the overwhelming conclusion is that aggression, jealousy, and strife require external stimuli for them to happen. We have done studies comparing prime-organisms on Shamym with those on planets of other close-in solar systems (**Rakiya, Kokav**, etc.) and have found major differences between planets.

These differences on adaptation to aggression, jealousy, and strife appear to be related to the processes of relationships between providers and birthers. For those planets on which providers and birthers have continuing relationships in reproducing, aggression is greater. There, higher levels of jealousy and strife and produced.

We were ignorant that these patterns could be trans-ferred to behaviors that were quite different than those associated with reproduction and relationships beyond the provider and birther interaction.

CHAPTER

FOUR

The Origin of Warlike Behavior

For over 50 million orbits, there was relative peace among and between us and our partners on the other planets. Then something serious happened and warfare broke out. Billions of Prime-Organisms on our planet and on 12 of our closest neighboring planets were killed in the resulting wars. Our scholars are still studying this phenomenon that led us to visit your planet and other planets. We identified Aretz as SS396 P3 (solar system 396/third planet from the mother star.)Later in this narrative, we will visit your solar system and I will encourage you to come along for your insights.

I asked him, *"Are you planning to bring me back to Aretz at the same time at which I found you?"*

He replied, **"Although we have not planned our return, we will take you to Aretz approximately 4,000 years before the time we first met."**

I was very upset with his plan, *"Do you mean I will never see my contemporaries from the time I left? My children, my grandchildren, my friends?"*

He said, **"Again, young man, be patient. We have ways of jumping time and we will return you to the time you were found. We will need your insights for the 4,000 years before you were born."**

Returning to the narrative, in total there were eight wars involving different groups of planets. But first, we will discuss wars, and all we have found out about what prompts them. Perhaps you can add to our knowledge.

Wars did not exist on Shamym. Our method of reproduction and the way we develop relationships is unique in our close-in universe. Since our methods of reproduction do not encourage having a partner as a permanent mate, we do not feel loyalty to any specific prime-organism. The organisms we parent do not stay with us, and neither do we establish mutual and permanent bonds of loyalty to our offspring. They are raised and assigned to a training program designed for the social good, then are selected to train for a specific work task. We view each other as having an important role in our civilization. Thus, we do not compete because we have nothing to vie for in our family and hence, no reason for competition.

The entire hierarchical organization of the prime-organisms of Shamym is based entirely on merit. Our leaders are selected by their virtue and aptitude. In moving up through each stage of our lives, the organisms selected for the next level are those that have the greatest merit and capability to fill the function.

Thus, even from **El Shadai** and his appointed leader **Nai** *(sometimes called Adonai),* to our functioning prime organisms, **Adam,** we accept the assignments and functions without conflict. This method of organization has produced a society where all perform to the best of their ability. Accordingly, our society can gather and produce enough gold for powering all other societies in our close-in universe, as well as provide adequate nourishment to enable each of us to survive.

"Aretz has many groups, called "nations" that have developed societies based upon different types of organization. Some of them are merit based, like your ruling leaders, others are based upon families, and others are based upon status and age."

Even aspects of our society that are dysfunctional, such as occasional cellular variations in a prime organism that results in the end of the life of the organism, are accepted as inevitable. The non-functioning prime organisms are replaced and the next most meritorious prime organism available continues the function of the deceased. Because of our rational, logical, and objective means of running our society, we have few reasons to be angry at each other. Our major problems arose in our contacts with other civilizations in our close-in universe.

In contrast the Shamym society, most of the Prime-Organisms on the solar system have produced societies with much more conflict. I have described two modes or reproducing organisms in other universes.

Rakiya is the planet that is closest to us. It has a mode of reproducing Prime-Organisms in which the providers and birthers have an ongoing relationship. Rakiyans have a system whereby providers and birthers mix the reproduction contributions in a vessel that maintains a specific temperature that helps these initial contributions combine.

At a specific stage in this process, the organism is moved to a sac inside the body of the birther. The prime organism develops inside the sac and is release when it can survive outside on its own. The birther is responsible for raising and educating the new prime organism (although programmed educational protocols are used to enhance the training.)

The provider and birther live with and guide the new prime organism, but might allow independent individuals to furnish comprehensive education in areas for which the organism is qualified. Depending upon the needs of society, provider and birther pairs are allowed to repeat this process several times.

Conflicts are common on Rakiya. Our scientists have suggested that the source of these issues relate to three factors.

First, the bond between provider and birther becomes very strong. Any attempt to interfere with the bond, whether by the society or by individuals in the society, causes secretion of a chemical in the thinking unit of the prime organism, causing increases in anger and aggression.

"We call this bond 'Marriage.'"

Second, the bonds between the provider/birther pair and the prime organism they have created become so strong that when an outside organism or groups of organisms interfere with the direction that the provider/birther desires for the offspring, a chemical is released in their thinking unit signaling a need for protection. This too has led to aggression and anger.

"On Earth, we have found a chemical in the brain we call Serotonin which is related to arguing."

Third, offspring of the same provider/birther pair see the other offspring of the pair as competition for sustenance and attention. The chemical that is secreted when this happens encourages anger along with a need to balance their perceived share of sustenance and attention. *"Like the humans of Aretz."*

Because of these three factors, Rakiya had many feuds, wars, and acts of anger and aggression. Some were within individual families, some were between clans made up of many family groupings, and some even expanded to other planets in the close-in universe. Examples of these acts will be described later in this History.

There were 12 planets on which provider/birther pairings were like those in Rakiya. The planets we have named that are like Rakiya, in that the provider and birther raise the new organism, include: *Alom, Yakom, Tayvel, Aiphot, Algabis* and *Matohr*, but there are others with which we have not made extensive contact. While these planets respect the rule of **El Shadai**, and yearn for the peace and cooperation that Shamym has, they do not expect me to be their ruler because their philosophy cannot adopt our strict rules where merit defines relationships and parents raise their new organisms.

"I must spend more time with you before I can remember these names. On Earth, there is a character in a fictional play about space travel called Mr. Spock who comes from a planet like

Shamym. In case you do not understand the concept of fiction, it means a life 'imagined' by an author."

The other planet close to us, **Kokav**, is one in which the process of transfer between the providers and birthers are related to a pleasurable experience. Typical of planets like Kokav, the provider/birther act of creating a prime organism is done several times by the same provider/birther pair and is repeated as many times as the pair desires to create a new organism. The pair of provider/birthers is very active in the maturation and education activities of the offspring, even calling upon specialists in their community to educate and help with maturation.

The planets with these types of reproduction systems generally have mutually complementary appendages which supply the two sets of organisms that combine to create the new prime organism. These appendages also provide the pleasurable experience.

Our scientists have found that since there is pleasure in the act of creating a new prime-organism, provider/birther pairs have found ways to experience the pleasure without combining the two sets of organisms used to create a new prime. We have also discovered that to experience the pleasure without creating a prime, pairs consisting of providers only and birthers only have become common.

"Aretz too has found that not all reproduction is done with males and females living together. Others use the act of reproduction for its pleasure alone with partners who may be male only, female only, or both sexes, but without a commitment for life."

El Shadai looked at me with a strange look.

Organisms on planets like Kokav are the most aggressive, jealous with the most strife in the universe. The reasons are like those of Rakiya with added issues.

Like Rakiya, on Kokav, the bond between provider and birther is extremely strong. This is because pleasure is associated with the provider/birther bond. Being able to create as many primes as they want and experiencing the pleasure both with and without the prime creation process strengthen the bond. An attempt to interfere or bond, whether by or with the society, or by individuals in the society, is more intensely felt. As with the Rakiyans, this causes secretion of a chemical in the thinking unit of the prime organism causing increases in anger and aggression. The level of the aggression has sometimes led to ending the life of a prime organism through jealousy.

"As I suggested, on Aretz, our healers have identified a chemical called Serotonin, which causes anxiety. This may convert to fear and aggression between and among humans that have high levels."

Like Rakiya, but with greater intensity, the bonds between the provider/birther pair and the prime organism they have created become extremely strong because the provider/birther pair is more involved with the prime they created. When an outside organism or groups of organisms interfere with the direction that the provider/birther desires for the offspring, a chemical is released in the thinking unit of the provider/birther signaling a need for protection. This too has led to aggression and anger.

As with the Rakiyans, offspring of the same provider/birther pair see the other offspring of the pair as competing with them for sustenance and attention. The chemical that is secreted when this happens encourages anger and a need to balance their perceived share of sustenance and attention. This is more intense in Kokav because of the greater involvement of the young prime with the provider/birther.

A fourth factor exists that is unique to planets like Kokav. With the ability to have the pleasurable experience of producing a prime without a birther, new levels of jealousy and conflict occurs between existing pairs and those that interlope into the singularity of the original pair. This has caused many conflicts and aggression upon prime organisms. There are several planets that have the same factors influencing the degree to which conflict and aggression lead to wars. We have named those planets with which we have learned most about; *Zalzul, Kinaha, Geniva, Bagida* and *Ratzah.* In our visit in your planet, we have found that these planets are like yours. We have named your planet *Aretz* because it is like these others.

CHAPTER
FIVE

The Role of the Thinking Unit on Emotions Leading to Warlike Behavior

Under the directions of El Shadai, we discovered that the instinct toward conflict and aggression (and ultimately war) rests in early family instincts of a civilization that reproduces and raises its offspring primes, and organizes its functions.

We have learned over time that the basic chemicals secreted to produce these aggressive emotions cause the same reactions when expanded to interactions between other organisms on the planet and on other planets.

"*Again, it appears that on Aretz this seems like Serotonin.*"

These reactions may be related to the SWOW principal. To be able to survive, all organisms – especially Prime-Organisms – must develop the instinct to survive. In doing so, the organisms are driven to minimize the impact of competing organisms on their existence.

If they have high levels of these chemicals and react to the competition of others, they are more likely to become stronger and survive.

"In Aretz, we have discovered, in my generation, that anger and competition turn-on instincts in the human called 'fight or flight.' This instinct readies the human muscles to defend. While dealing with their own anger and competition, their muscles ache, passing through this instinct. Some of our scientists call this process 'frustration-aggression' symptom."

"On our planet, Shamym, under my rule, these reactions are minimized because all the functions of our planet are planned and specified by a rigid set of rules. Our belief in the system of survival and the role defined for us is based on merit."

Except for a small proportion of Prime-Organisms that were defective in the formation of their processing organ, all of us have developed without the need or behavior of conflict or aggression. However, we were not properly prepared for how planets in our close-in universe would respond to us. This turned out to be harmful for us, but an experience that honed our belief about what we must do in our attempt to perfect the universe.

CHAPTER
SIX

The Story of the Matohr Civil War
The War of the False Promises

Matohr is a planet that takes a travel time of five of our solar oribits to reach from Shamym. The light from Matohr takes one fiftieth of an orbit period to reach us. As indicated previously, Matohr has a mode of reproducing Prime-Organisms in which the providers and birthers have an ongoing relationship. With their system, providers and birthers mix the reproduction contributions in a vessel that maintains a specific temperature to help the initial contributions combine.

"In Aretz, many groups of medical experts have developed a similar process called in-vitro reproduction."

At a specific stage in this combination, the new organism is moved to a sac inside the body of the birther. *"Like the Aretz experiments."*

The prime organism develops inside the sac and is released when it can survive outside this protection. The birther is responsible for raising and educating the new prime organism (although under my rules, programmed educational protocols may be used.)

The provider and birther live with and guide the new prime organism, but might allow independent groups to offer comprehensive education in areas for which the organism is qualified. Depending upon the needs of society, provider and birther pairs can repeat this process several times.

Here too, conflicts are common on planets like Matohr and they are related to three factors. First, the bond between provider and birther becomes very strong. Any attempt to interfere with the bond, whether by the society or by individuals, causes secretion of the anger and aggression chemical in the thinking unit of the prime organism.

The bonds between the provider/birther pair and the prime organism they have created become so strong that when outside creatures interfere with the direction that the provider/birther desire for the offspring, they respond to the chemical in their thinking unit, signaling a need for protection of their young. This too has led to aggression and anger.

The offspring of the same provider/birther pair see their siblings as competition for sustenance and attention. The chemical that is secreted when this happens promotes anger **(again Serotonin?)** and a need to balance their perceived share of attention within the family unit.

Thus, of these three factors, Matohr has had many feuds, wars, and acts of anger and aggression. Some were within individual families, some were between clans made up of many family groupings, and some even expanded to other planets in the close-in universe.

"In certain groupings on Aretz, the formations of clans are common. In a nation in the middle of our western hemisphere, two clans, the Hatfields and McCoys, fought each other for 100 years."

By the decree pronounced by **El Shadai**, we convinced the leaders of Matohr to limit the hostility by selecting a strong omnipotent leader who would create strict rules against feuds and disagreements. The leader and his ruling council studied the origin of feuds, wars, and acts of anger. They found that many of these issues in the new organisms were as a result of the way in which they were brought up as siblings. This act of living together caused inbred jealousy, which became serious as the organism matured.

Another factor contributing to these fights was the jealousy between birthers and providers. Many birthers wanted to seek different providers and their prime provider secreted the same anger and jealousy chemical. In the same way, providers wanted to reproduce with other birthers, which made the birthers jealous and angry.

"Another common issue in Aretz."

With complete authority over the population, the leader I had chosen, and his council, created a series of laws that had a major impact on the populations and led to a major revolution. Since the birthers and Providers struggled with anger and jealousy, the first law was that upon the birth of an offspring organism, the birthers and providers were required to separate and go to a different location and a different work function. The offspring organism was taken over by a leader council and placed into a learning environment separate from their "parents." In effect, this law forced upon them the method that Shamym used regarding different ways of reproducing.

It required the leader to advise parents to live separately in two distinct communities, one made up of only providers and the other made up of only birthers. Schools run by the leader and his council had the responsibility to raise the offspring born to provider-birther pairs. They were educated, trained, and when they reached the age at which they could reproduce, they were put into the community in which they fit. In this community, they learned a function and when needed, they were combined with an opposite person to become a provider/birther pair.

This approach had a beneficial effect. The Leadership Council had developed and conducted research on the characteristics of organisms that could be predicted before birth. They found that other nearby planets had identified a spiral band that contained cells that influenced the attributes and personalities of each organism. They also found that the mixture of the cells of the provider and birther pair influenced the makeup of their offspring. I developed a program to map each offspring on the characteristics of their spiral cells. The leader ordained that if the planet needed new offspring that required certain skills, characteristics, and emotions, a provider/birther pair would be selected and matched to provide the offspring needed.

"On Aretz, many nations avoid planned upbringing and genetic manipulation. There were several nations, including the largest on Earth (China), that attempted to manipulate the sex and genes of new humans. But it was found by many that the randomness

of life produces humans that have more complex brains (or as you would say, thinking units.")

For the first seventeen years that the Matohr ruling leader was in power, his decision to change the process of mating, living, and forming familial groups appeared to be working well. Violence, jealousy, and anger virtually disappeared. I say "virtually" because within the communities of solely providers and solely birthers, new interactions occurred that were like provider/birther relationships. In the beginning, the leader thought that these types of relationships were an abomination. But I convinced the leader to soften his objection to these relationships when he observed that the provider/provider and birther/birther bonds led to a life of satisfaction and a good way to tamp down on the unhappiness of not being without opposite sex organisms. When the need for birthers and providers to join to create a prime offspring (selected by the rules of the leadership group) they were chosen based upon the match of spiral cells. When they finished the task and the offspring was born, they returned to their pairs and the offspring was sent to the training and education facility run by the leadership council.

Social bonds were created among the offspring who were placed into training groups until their maturity. Because the training and maturity teaching of offspring were done in a collaborative way, conflict among them was minimized.

Even so, the Matohr Civil War emerged from this apparently ideal environment. For much of the history of Matohr, the organisms accepted the concept and belief of El Shadai and the omnipotent leader, El Shadai, who was also called **Adonai**. They prayed to this leader, offered him gifts, and called him, **My Master**. They followed his laws and approaches to the organization of the providers, birthers, and offspring as a basic law of peaceful existence.

But the organization of the three groups of organisms – birthers only, providers only, and offspring only – created new ways of coming together. Apparently, the stimulus of friendships across provider/birther pairs set off a specific set of chemicals in the thinking unit that gave the pairs higher satisfaction. Without these chemicals, the communities of birthers and providers experimented with other stimuli to take the place of the chemicals.

Birther environments held regular gatherings in which experiences were reported. Originally, these gatherings were used to exchange information and discuss occurences involving group interaction. As time went on, birthers sought different ways of communicating their experiences and interactions. In the beginning, the group spoke to each other with words and concepts that sounded like the other words and concepts that had come before it. In visits to your planet we found that your organisms had done a similar thing and called it "rhyming."

Over time, the group members found pleasure in setting their communication sounds in a way that changed the tone and speed at which each sound is uttered. In your planet, there is an approach similar to this that you call "singing." Some of the tones used to sing the communication were further developed so that words were not necessary any longer. The tone and speed were reproduced without the words. But with familiarity to the singing, the tones and speed were easily converted in the mind to the words.

"The emergence of poetry and music on Aretz is an area with which I am not familiar. The Matohr experience might be similar to

how it originated on Aretz. We know that other organisms in Aretz had pictures of devices that could have made musical notes. The Matohr experiences suggests that the growth of rhyming and music emerged from social interactions."

In time, the birthers found that silicon, a substance that is plentiful on the planet, could be melted, strung into cords and reeds, and plucked by the manipulative organ of the body. The sounds that were reproduced in singing could be duplicated by the cords of silicon. This product produced a phenomenon, which you call "music." Various instruments of music were developed based upon the type of sound desired. Some did not play the music, but the rhythm of the music by using instruments that were hit against each other to the beat. In our travels to many planets, we had never seen music as an experience except when we came to explore your planet, Aretz. Your planet is considered to have one of the highest functioning prime organisms along with our planets, Shamym and Matohr.

Initially, the methods at which experiences and interactions were exchanged among group members were limited to poetry, rhyming, singing, and music. One day, a birther, seeking a more intense way in which to communicate feelings, attempted to use her organ of visual sensing (eye) and picked up a thin rod that had been burnt. She rubbed it against a piece of parchment that came from the dried remains of the outer skin of a dead organism used for food. Over time, this birther could represent by sight the experience and interactions that she had sensed. In many cases, it was different from the actual experience and interaction. Those birthers in her group found that the visual representation of the experience and interaction contained more emotion and feeling than did the words, rhymes, songs, and music that described the experience.

"Aural arts such as music, poetry, and sounds apparently crossed over to the visual arts. These behaviors expanded the artistic output of the prime organisms and created a unique universal way of sharing feelings and emotions."

Over time, the birther population found out about these new ways of communicating to each other and schools were set up to practice and share these new forms of communication. Eventually, the birther population spent more effort on these forms of communication then they did on the belief system of the planet and the importance the omnipotent leader. Soon, the birther population forgot the rules and regulations. When birthers were asked to produce a copy of an organism of a certain type they refused. All their time was being spent in source music rhymes and art. The birther population no longer became productive in their work tasks. Output declined and the education of birthers in certain skills needed by the omnipotent leader and the council ceased.

Birthers began to compete for implements to improve their singing, music, and art. Materials used in these skills ran into shortages. For the first time in the history of the planet, birthers began fighting with each other. Those who controlled the supply of these materials benefited materially. During the competition between suppliers, physical violence was common, leading to the deaths and injuries of many thousand birthers. Again, the rules of the omnipotent leader and his counsel were forgotten and ignored.

"For this kind of behavior to be of value it must not be the target of hatred and dominance."

The provider population of the planet developed a similar behavior. Providers met in meetings and shared with each other their experiences and life. Since providers appear to have a less emotional response programmed into their spiral band than do the birthers, they used more physical and spatial methods to share their lives.

At first, providers developed games in which they acted out their experiences and interactions. Over time, they turned their games into competitive contests. Subsets of providers were formed and each reenacted the group experience and interaction, with the better one evaluated by an impartial judge. Providers created games that were analogies to their experiences. Ultimately, the better performing providers were given the opportunity to compete with other capable providers. Their performance was viewed by an audience of providers and assessed by the most experienced judges.

Much time was used viewing these contests. During each competition, impartial judges were used to score the ability of each team to complete its experiences and life stories. Since different groups of providers who favored different teams had emotional attachments to their team, arguments broke out between the teams, the judges, and the viewers. These arguments sometimes became violent as judges were beaten or, in some cases, murdered, and fighting broke out between the viewers who preferred each team. Many providers began devoting their time to these games and competitions. Forgotten by the providers were the memory and rules of the omnipotent leader. On certain days, the providers spent their time viewing contests between the best teams. When judges made decisions that were not favorable, armies of providers were organized and battles ensued between viewers that favored one team or another.

It is estimated that these battles cost over one million lives of provider organisms. Ignorance of the teachings of the omnipotent leader caused breakdowns in civil behavior and adherence to the universal laws, promulgated by the omnipotent leader and the ruling council.

There was a breakdown of planning on the planet. With El Shadai's recommendations, the omnipotent leader and ruling council declared a state of emergency. During the period when the birthers and providers developed the use of games and abstract representations to communicate with each other and pass the time, planning for the development of new and young organisms was delayed. The time necessary to resolve the right provider with a proper birther delayed the process. Apparently the years in which providers and birthers were distracted by this idle time, a shortage arose of new Prime-Organisms to fill important functions on the planet. This problem, in and of itself, would have been solved naturally, but the loss of life associated with these activities had eliminated many birthers and providers that possessed desirable genetic characteristics for the next generation.

Faced with this insurrection, El Shadai and the omnipotent leader, Adonai, suggested to his ruling council to outlaw the activities of the providers and birthers, and they agreed. Since these activities were ingrained into these organisms, they used their competitive skills to revolt against the restrictions imposed upon them by the leader and his council. Small groups of providers and birthers began to work together to overthrow the powers that be. Owning the ability to organize the society, the leader and council formed groups of trained organisms to combat attempts to overthrow the ruling council.

The battles that raged went far beyond the expectations of either side of the conflict. Providers and birthers attacked the places in which the leader and council met. Originally, these attacks were planned to reduce the efficiency of the leader and council to administer to the needs of the planet. What happened is that the defense of the administration group required more violent responses that had been imagined by either group. Each side developed weapons that, while originally meant to scare the other side away, were used to disable organisms from the other side.

The chemicals secreted to promote aggression and hatred resulted in more dangerous weapons. These weapons were designed to injure the thinking mechanism of the enemy organism, the organs of manipulation, and the organs of locomotion. In many cases, the use of these weapons by either side became fatal. It was estimated that 500,000 members of the provider and birther groups lost their lives in this insurrection. The Adonai and his Council's army lost 250,000 organisms. Because of the violent battles and the ability of the leader and his council to regain control, the birther and provider groups agreed to respect the needs of the omnipotent leader in return for him easing his requirements for them.

It took Matohr many years for the planet to return to its productive level. They reported to the neighboring planets in the solar system what had happened and what could be learned from this insurrection in hopes that the violence that occurred in Matohr would not be repeated on other planets. An interplanetary council was organized to develop rules that could be applied to the planetary group to prevent this from happening again.

El Shadai summoned groups of sages from each planet to review the history of this violence. They decided that the lesson to be learned was that when there is an omnipotent leader and council acting in the best interests of the planet, their prime organisms must not take up interests and distractions that are put ahead of the commands and interests of the leader and his council. In effect, these activities took the place of the leaders and council, and became more important to the organisms. They provided an environment in which the omnipotent leader was ignored and even disrespected as these interests and activities became central to the lives of the provider and birther population. The rule that was developed was:

Rule 1:

An omnipotent leader acting in the interest of his people must be obeyed and respected. No activities or distraction that substitute for or lesser respect for the omnipotent leader shall be taken up. The organisms may practice activities and distractions but they must not be placed ahead of the leader, nor used to reduce the importance or authority of the leader.

CHAPTER
SEVEN

The Nakom Rebellion
The War of the False Leaders

There are several planets with prime organisms in our solar system and close-in galaxies that have developed a variety of life forms. These include intellectually superior organisms, organisms with minimal intelligence but skills in manipulation and motion, and some with few skills and little knowledge – in effect, a non-thinking organism. Through the SWOW mechanism, these varieties of life forms are strongly dependent upon the planet size, its distance from the sun, and the resulting impact of these factors on the gravitational and temperature sources of the particular planet. Many planets have developed no life because these factors exceeded the ability of a potential prime organism to survive.

Nakom was a planet in our solar system, but its population was close to the limits of survival. Its size was 20,000 miles in diameter (32,000 km) and it was 200,000,000 miles from its sun (322 million km). Its sun was large enough for it to receive minimal heat for part of its rotation, but by the standards of Shamym and your planet, Aretz, it would be an inhospitable environment – constantly below the freezing point of water (bi-hydrous oxide), and even lower temperatures for a good part of its rotation around the sun. Yet Prime-Organisms did develop in this environment, and those that survived and adapted to Nakom were quite different than others in the close-in universe.

When Shamym visited the planet, it was found that the SWOW mechanism was influential. Because of the gravitational force of the planet and the cold temperatures, the Prime-Organisms of Nakom were muscular and had an outer coat covered with fur. Surviving on a planet with a large diameter produces muscular development favoring those who can move in an environment of heavy gravity. These were prime organisms that could walk erect when moving through a dangerous environment so that their line of vision and the position of its manipulative organs could be brought into play if defense was needed. But for most of their time when passing through familiar environments – for both speed of locomotion and comfort in moving – they used both their locomotive organs (feet) and manipulative organs (hands) to move in a rapid "gallop." During this type of locomotion, they retracted their finer manipulative appendages (fingers) so as not to damage them. The cold temperatures favored a fur-covered body to survive.

Their survival was aided by rapid metabolism. Their food intake consisted of eating fast and often, their circulation organs could process large amounts of body fluid, and their intake of the thin oxygen on the planet was accomplished with many hyper breaths in well-developed lungs.

The planet developed into the type on which birthers and providers had a permanent relationship and reproduction was of a pleasurable experience. Once an organism was born to the birther/ provider pair, it lived with its parents until independent enough to move on to its own relationship. Our scientists have discovered with these types of families, competition between organisms is developed within social groupings that reside near each other and in tribal groups within communities of tribes.

The population of Nakom was not considered intelligent by the inhabitants of those planets in the close-in solar system that could travel there and interact with them. Our scientists have found that the ability to develop thinking and reasoning unit is a function of the availability of high quality protein that could be ingested by the prime organism. Since Nakom had very low temperatures, its surface was inhospitable to inferior species. Those that were water-borne could supply protein but had a limited life span as the water covering Nakom was in its solid state most of the time. There was but a short period during which waterborne nutrients were available, but it was not long enough for adequate volumes of protein to be consumed. The other source of protein was land born organisms and species. But these species were even more disadvantaged than the Prime-Organisms because they had less capacity for finding and tracking waterborne protein.

Their way of surviving through the SWOW method was to take the process literally – the stronger organisms fought and over-took the weaker specimens among them and used their bodies for food. The prime organisms joined forces to hunt, kill, and eat the many non-Prime-Organisms to ingest as much protein as they could. But these amounts were much below the protein consumptions of species on other planets.

Over many eons of time, Nakom primes became great manipulators of objects, but were not strong in reasoning and planning. In effect, they became a planet that developed skills in carving and assembly of objects comprised of a variety of materials. They could not develop interplanetary travel so they were forever trapped in the Nakom environment because of their inability to reason and design complex machinery.

Based on my command, other planets of the solar systems visited and studied Nakom. They saw in Nakom primes skills required for their planet's manufacturing which they were unable to do themselves. They integrated the Nakom society into the family of planets and gave them the task of carving and constructing units that could be used for living, aesthetics, and modes of transportation. They presented the Nakom primes with plans and encouraged them to use these to build and manufacture what the other planets could not.

My planet, Shamym, was the leader in mining and in using gold that was processed for other planets as fuel for interplanetary travel. (I will describe later in this document a major war in which we suffered greatly because of our need of a consistent gold supply.) Other planets such as Rakiya, Zalzul, Kinaha, Geniva, Bagida and Ratzah also participated in interplanetary trade on such materials as silver, copper, granite, platinum, uranium, wood, and other elements. These elements were used or converted into other objects and mechanisms. For these planets, Nakom was an ideal trading partner.

The Prime-Organisms of Nakom were good at finishing a product or process using their limited skills to the exact specifications of the planet that supplied a basic material. For example, Rakiya had one of the largest supplies of raw silver in the universe. The scientists of Rakiya found that raw silver ore could be polished and mounted in units so that when exposed to the light of its sun, could generate enough power to supply its energy needs. Raw silver was extracted from its ore and made into silver squares. These squares were sent to Nakom where they were mounted in granite frames and connected to groups of 128 squares where the energy of any pair of two squares would be increased to the power of six.

"How were fees for work applied between different planets?"

Rakiya compensated Nakom by sending them plants from its agricultural output for which Nakom's surface was too cold for growth. Rakiya would further compensate Nakom with food to supply its population, and permit Nakom to use approximately 10 percent of its energy output for its own purposes.

For many eons, the primes of Nakom developed their skills. However, with a population of Prime-Organisms with limited intelligence, the inability to travel and expand their interests, and their lack of contact with other species, they began to look inward for their activities.

As the head of the solar system, I appointed a leader, **Avod,** as the leader of the Nakom planet. Avod was not a single prime but the name of the leader's position on the planet. Along with a ruling council of 125 **Avodim,** Avod set the laws of Nakom. I appointed the leader and council members.

At an early age, the working population of Nakom was assigned to various jog functions to work under masters of the craft. These functions included carving stones and other mineral matter, carving hard vegetable matter, drawing objects on a flat surface, and molding materials into shapes. The best members of the population in each function were assigned to work groups, which they contributed to the success of Nakom.

Assignment to a workgroup meant that the worker performed a certain type of craft task repeatedly. The lower levels of intelligence of the prime organisms enabled them to tolerate these repeated tasks. Our scientists had discovered in studies of various planetary organisms, that those of higher intelligence were more curious than those of lower intellect. Repeated tasks by the intelligent organisms would lead to a state of anomie or boredom. This would make them unhappy with their work roles and reduce their effectiveness on the tasks in which they specialized. The lower level of intelligence of Nakom primes meant that they would be loyal to their tasks for their entire life. At a certain point in their life, they would be allowed to end their work requirement and live the rest of their life in rest and relaxation.

Many of the older workers would use their leisure time to continue to practice their craft skills. Those that worked with metal made figurines and designs. Stone workers crafted stones into designs that were carved out of rocks. Those that painted flat surfaces experimented with new materials and surfaces. Each group of artists perfected their skills after they left full-time work behind. Our scientists believe that this greater creativity occurred because, for the first time in their lives, they were not asked to use their skills to manufacture what were the specifications of others. Studies by our scientists found that the brain size of the Nakom workers increased when they went into their time of rest and relaxation. Of course, even this enhanced size was small compared to that of other primes on other planets.

Part of their creative efforts dealt with which subject matters they should represent. At first, they used it to reproduce everyday aticles such as tools, family objects used for locomotion, hygiene, raising and training young primes in their families, etc. Over time, they began reproducing models of live objects such as water creatures and lower forms of land creatures. These included some who had become domesticated and lived in the proximity of primes. They were used for companionship and work. One animal, the **Sooss,** was used to pull heavy weights – too heavy for the primes to pull themselves.

Aware of the animal, I asked El Shadai a question, *"One group of my people on Earth have used the word Sooss as a name for what we call Horse. Is it possible they might have learned it by your visits to Aretz?*

El Shadai said, **"True. We often interacted with people in Aretz, but they were not aware of our science. They may have written about us as a ruler or deity."**

The older primes prided themselves in their abilities and the output of their skills. They learned how to perfect skills they had and apply them across subject matter and materials. The primes of Nakom were competitive and it didn't take long to turn their work into contests.

Not limited to using their skills to do the repetitive crafts specified by others, they began exploring new ways of using the materials and talents they had. As an example, a prime who was an accomplished carver would try different tools for sculpting. With these tools, carved objects could have rough finishes, smooth surfaces, a surface made up of tiny images, a surface created by small dots, etc. The types of materials used could multiply these differences. Some surfaces were made of hydrocarbon materials that grew, made up of tiny cells. Other materials were made of metals used in other projects – gold, silver, iron, platinum, iridium, and other elemental metals. So, when the variety of carving methods were multiplied by the many types of surfaces they worked on, there were thousands of techniques that could be classified.

A second type of craft practiced was by applying a series of liquid colors to a flat surface. These colors and dyes could be made of many combinations. The most common was an elemental powder combined with a liquid. This liquid could be water, oils, bodily fluids, animal excretions, and melted elements. As with the carving artists, those who used these techniques chose many surfaces on which to apply these colors, including woven fabrics, dried skin of dead organisms, surfaces of hydrocarbons, surfaces of elements (like those used for carving), and surfaces of the planet including rocks and dirt. As with those who carved, there were thousands of combinations they could use in this art form.

It wasn't long before the older primes found that they could combine these two techniques by assembling both three dimensional with two-dimensional crafts. The addition of combining these two types of crafts added many thousands of combinations of art assemblies. The challenges and interest that these older crafts workers had when they had thousands of alternatives they could work with rose steadily. And it was all without the previous constrictions they had in their youth when all the work they did was limited to the specific specifications and methods required by the contracting planet

For hundreds of Nakom years, older primes created many different craft objects. New generations of these older primes continued with their efforts, freed from the need to create what those on other planets needed. By the process of SWOW, the most exciting crafts came into being. Mind you, contributing to the support of the planet by making crafts required by more advanced planets were still the essential task of Prime-Organisms, for their work supported the planet of Nakom with food, clothing, and housing. The Avod of Nakom made assignments, governed the population makeup, and contacted the planets for which the work was done. The Avod was kind to the people of Nakom and made sure that the balance of work on the planet was not damaged.

"Like Aretz, the primes of Nakom developed a system of creating art. I am not sure how Aretz developed art but it is likely to have been similar to your experience."

But over time, things began to change. Millions of prime organisms were working to manufacture items used by other planets from specifications sent to them. The success of Nakom grew. The Avod (and his group of Avodim) was managing so many functions that it was necessary to delegate some of these to others.

Before long, the contacts of any work group was an assistant Avod many levels below that of the supreme Avod. These assistants were called **Seraphim.** They did their best to keep the workers and crafters happy and satisfied while meeting difficult schedules. The workers and crafters were in family units that contained older primes who were using their skills for their own pleasures, creating new things based upon their own creative abilities.

The beginning of a chaotic situation was developing. The worker primes had lost direct contact with the Avod and his counselors. They were overworked trying to meet their deadlines. Their orders and rules were coming from a substitute for the Avod. They were not provided with satisfaction that originated in their thinking unit. Their contact with the older primes left them with a feeling of incompleteness. The older primes were doing work and crafts that provided them with great pleasure and satisfaction, but they were not contributing to the planet. The younger primes expressed their problems to the older primes. They blamed their unhappiness on having no contact with Avod. Their inability to have contact did not allow them to revere the leader. Family unions all over the planet faced similar problems.

Older primes, who were well respected, met to discuss this issue. How could they bring the Avod back into the lives of the younger primes? Councils of older primes met across the planet. They offered solutions as varied as the geography of the planet. Some suggested having the Avod visit each of the 3,700 workplaces. However, the number of workplaces and the time available to the Avod made this impossible. Another solution offered was to send one representative of each work group to meet with the Avodim. This was done several times but the ability of the Avod to personally connect to any one representative was poor. Even more important, the representatives were unable to even get close to the Avod and this left them nearly as frustrated and unhappy as they were before these solutions were developed.

The older primes met with the technologically advanced planets, such as Shamym and Kokav, to discuss how they might solve this problem. These planets had developed a technology of three-dimensional holograms that enabled a life-sized three-dimensional image to be transferred over long distances. Using trading credits from these provider planets, they bartered for 3,700 receiver units and one transmission unit.

For 95 of our years, the groups of prime crafters met regularly with the image of the Avod and participated in gatherings in which the leader spoke to them and urged them on with their workloads. During this time, the Avod changed as the previous one retired from his task. As many of the prime craftsmen also aged, they began experimenting with new forms of unfettered art. But over time, the newer generations of craftsmen grew distant from the Avod, who they only knew through the holographic projection. And as with the previous generation, they became dissatisfied with their workload and rebelled against their stern work tasks and the ways in which they were forced to carry these duties out. In doing so, they did not meet their quotas and schedules. The elder craftsmen, aware that this rebellion was a result of the absence of the Avod, sought a way to find a meaningful substitute for him.

They developed the idea to use the creativity they had developed to generate an image of the Avod as a substitute for the real Avod. Using the variety of art forms they had perfected, they utilized their skills to represent the unseen Avod. Those that worked in three-dimensional art forms began sculpting images of the Avod. Over time, these images evolved to three types: ultra-realistic, where the image was an exact reproduction of the Avod; abstract-realistic which was, an outgrowth of the need expressed to introduce the emotion of love and dependence into the image of the Avod; and fully-abstract where the emotions and love of the Avod were represented, absent of the real image of Avod. The elder crafters produced these images in three dimension, two-dimensional, and a mixture of three and two-dimensional.

Over time and generations, the work of the crafters became better and better. But the distance between the actual Avod and the crafters became further and further away from each other. While work quality and satisfaction with it went up, the relationship with the Avod and other benefits deteriorated.

After hundreds of Nakom years, the workers felt that they no longer needed Avod and his council. They set their own schedules, refused to accept the workloads, and formed independent congregations to supervise their own work. When the Avod and his council of Avodim saw that they could not run the planet because they had lost control of the working primes, they sent representative to see them. The worker primes expelled these envoys.

But the worker primes were also not united. In accepting the objects that represented Avod, some strongly felt that those that were realistic were the best portrayal. They formed separate congregations who preferred the realistic representation of Avod. Over time, members of this group began setting their own priorities and work schedules.

Other worker primes preferred the abstract realist representation of Avod. These primes were more moved by the emotion of love and dependence they saw in the image of the Avod. They too formed separate congregations and set their own schedules and priorities for work.

A third group of worker primes formed congregations based upon fully abstract representation of Avod. They also united in setting their own work priorities.

In the beginning of this movement, there were minor differences in philosophy between the three groups. But over time, the opinions of each group began to harden.

Our scientists have found that when, and if, different belief systems conflict with each other, there is a possibility of strife. This emerges from two sources. If the belief systems are competing for membership, each will try to increase their beliefs **at the expense of the other's beliefs**. This conflict often outweighs filial attachments each has with others and leads to frustration and clarity in communicating to each other. A term in your language that describes this is **"Subsessionism."** Frustration, the inability to fulfill a goal, often leads to aggression. The likelihood of aggression is greatest in organisms with lower forms of intelligence, for intelligence his highly related to weighing knowledge before deciding on any action. The process of weighing knowledge requires scanning with your thinking organ all types of information with which one may agree or disagree. The process of scanning both sides gives you empathy with those you may disagree with. Understanding frustration reduces conflict.

"It is unbelievable that in a distant planet from Aretz called Nakom, in a solar system we could never even reach, the concept of subsessionism reeked its terrible results. Oh, if only we in Aretz had seen this and learned about it. I first found out about it from Father James Carroll. But it was too late in history to save millions

of lives. Father Carroll opened the historical book in which people of different religions fought and killed people of opposite beliefs. So Christians fought Jews, Islamists fought Christians, Christians fought Islamists, and Jews fought Arabs. And all of these wars could have been prevented had each one loved their God as much as they could have loved others who God created. But the God all of them believed in was a force they could only imagine. I may be the only person besides Moses and the Prophets that have travelled with God – El Shadai. "

Since Nakom was not a planet of highly intelligent prime organisms, the three groups of workers – realists, abstract-realists, and fully-abstract – developed significant disagreements with each other. The Avod and council of Avodim also objected to their loss of discipline of the three groups. It became impossible for the Avod to set quotas for the economy to succeed. Without productivity, Nakom was unable to import materials to manufacture and foodstuffs for their storage.

It was not long before the Avod summoned his council of 125 Avodim to discuss how to rectify the economic damage being caused by the work delays and stoppages. The council had traditionally been a peaceful group whose main function in Nakom was to satisfy the needs of both the crafts primes and the economic planners of Nakom. The planners, however, were unable to manage the planet without the work of the crafts primes. They had developed a protection force of Prime-Organisms especially chosen from the population, based upon a rigorous way of identifying, in the early period of life, the existence of specific skills including strength, endurance, and courage. It turned out that these skills were the inverse of the skills of the craft primes – creativity, fine manual manipulation, and color mixing. Only 10 percent of the population of Nakom qualified for the protection force, but their skills in conflict resolution would overcome the nine to one advantage of the size of the craft primes. The planners were not easily convinced in the use of the protection force to solve this problem, so they were slow to authorize them to take action. It took the time for half of a revolution of the planet around the mother star for a decision to be made.

The planners asked the Avod and his council to send an ultimatum to the craft leaders to return to work. When it was received, there were mixed responses, based upon the skill sets of the craft prime groupings. The realist group gathered its council and debated what they should do. After several contentious meetings throughout the planet, the realists were open to accepting this ultimatum. It seemed that along with their preference for realism in their artistic skills came a preference for acceptance of realism and logic in life. They immediately sensed that the Avod and his council were serious and if they refused their request, they would use the protection force against them.

However, all did not go well with the other two crafts groups. Both the abstract-realists and the fully-abstract groups, in their own closed meetings, were not supportive of the offers of the Avod and his council. Over the course of the work stoppage, both groups experienced immense happiness from their freedom of expression. Returning to work would require them to subvert their newfound expression in crafts, and return to the task of carrying out the work contract to be done exactly as it was specified by the contracting planet and supervised by the worker's council of Avodim.

The willingness of the realist craftspeople to return to work caused a rift within the crafts community. Even if they had returned to work, they could not have met the quotas and requirements of the planet. Unable to fill the contracts from the supplier planets, the work would be transferred to other working planets. The council of the Avodim asked the ruling government to bring their strength and armies into the fray. Initially, the intervention of the government consisted of ultimatums to the strikers and threats of whatever force they could bring against them until they relented.

At first, the striking crafts groups did not take these ultimatums and threats seriously. For thousands of cycles around the sun, Nakom had been a passive planet with little violence. When work and crafts are held in high esteem, organisms, with few exceptions, refrain from violence. But with the growing absence of work, the loss of income and food sources, and craft workers set against each other, the very survival of families and organisms were at risk.

It all started when a group of realist craft artists broke into a council meeting of abstract realists and argued with its members about why the strike must end. They contended that the image of the Avod must be realistic. That using abstract images of the Avod was not acceptable. The argument became heated as each side expressed its feelings. And remember, many of the crafters who belonged to different "schools" might have been blood relatives who grew up together and shared the same providers and birthers.

Let it be known that our scientific experts have found that each prime organism has many needs. The importance of these needs change as the prime organism goes through its life stages. When the prime organism is first born and dependent upon parents and family for sustenance and protection, the family and its security is a primary need. But as the Prime-Organisms enter a craft group and may become a birther or provider of new primes, its interests and needs move toward sustaining its own close knit family.

Since the strike impacted the viability of each prime's family and craft group, it no longer shared the needs of those primes that may have been in their family. The arguments between the various craft groups occasionally broke out into physical confrontations. When word of this reached the council of Avodim, they requested governing forces to intervene in a way to stop the violence.

The council of Avodim met for several rotations of the planet. The discussion was heated, as the primary goal of this operation was to bring the workers back to work with minimal effort or coercion. It was decided that an emissary should communicate clearly to the workers what damage the work stoppage was bringing Nakom, and why they should return to their tasks quickly.

I called together a council and using my name. El Shadai, the council sent one of their best emissaries, known for his calm demeanor. His name was Salem. The working group to convince them to return to work welcomed Salem. At the time in which this occurred, it was not common for those in the council, like Salem, to attempt to understand the details and opinions of those he had to convince. The governing council ruled by fiat where the carefully thought out policies of the council were decided without taking into consideration the opinions of those they ruled.

Salem's discussion with the carefully organized striking craft groups dwelled upon all the reasons they must return to work: the economy of the planet, the need to complete the work to earn the food supplies, and the importance of these to the Avod. At no time was he sensitive to or knowledgeable of the reasons the striking workers were aggrieved. Had he asked them for the reasons they were striking, they would have explained it all to him in a peaceful manner. Yet every time a crafts person spoke up, he replied with, "We will consider what you think, but we cannot act upon it." This passive and peaceful behavior on his part only frustrated the crafts people he was sent to negotiate with. In this document I have often mentioned the responses of Prime-Organisms to frustration. It was in no one's imagination that Salem would frustrate the crafts organisms. Yet apparently, acknowledgment without action could be a source of frustration, but not universally so.

"On Aretz, the rules of many groups are to negotiate and bargain when they disagree with each other. Salem did not negotiate. A true negotiation permits each side to hear the opinions of the other side."

A meeting was called in a place where hundreds of Prime-Organisms gathered. These attendees were proud of their crafts and desired to have control over their lives. A single crafts person, by the name of Meshug, lost control of his frustration and tried to assuage it with a physical attack on Salem. Meshug picked up a piece of an abstract image of Avod made of lead, the material that protects organisms from the radiation of the sun. He had brought this object to the meeting to show Salem an example of his work. In his frustration, he threw it in the direction of Salem. The missive of lead was seen to fly over the heads of the attendees in the direction of Salem. The art work Meshug lovingly created for Avod struck Salem in his thinking unit and Salem immediately ceased living, his thinking unit crushed beyond repair.

"In recent times, experts in psychology, the science of the mind, believe that the feeling of frustration is often followed by aggression."

The room was struck silent. The crafts primes were upset, for Salem was a representative of the beloved Avod. In sadness, they carefully wrapped the remains that were once Salem, placed it in an outer container made of gold, and a delegation of 10 senior crafts-people escorted the body to the council of Avodim. Meanwhile, as their structure required, the perpetrator of this action, Meshug, was taken to be hidden in a secret place. A group of guards was sent to protect his location and his physical form and body.

The council of Avodim was struck by sadness when they saw the remains of Salem. They asked the delegation to identify and return the prime organism who had killed Salem so that he could be punished. The delegation refused to identify Meshug. They explained that the crafts primes had an organization in which the unity of the group precludes any one person from being punished for an act that is committed in the presence of the whole group. The whole group must accept the responsibility for the acts of one of its members. The council detained the delegation and queried them for a long time, trying to convince them to divulge the name and location of the prime who had damaged Salem and caused him to cease living. The delegation remained steadfast in their belief of staying silent. In desperation, the council ordered the delegation be detained and an army of 20,000 was dispatched to the crafts organisms to meet with the craft primes and seek out the perpetrator of the violent act.

When the crafts group received the message that their delegation was being detained and an army was being dispatched, they instituted their emergency protocol. This seldom-used move had been developed many eons before and used when there was a threat to the population. All three crafts groups, two of which were not even involved in the Salem meeting, joined them in the common threat to their craft society. A group of 8,000 craft prime organisms had been formed and trained in the arts of overpowering an attacking group. One hundred of them went to the place in which Meshug was hidden to protect him. The remaining group hid in the area a short distance from the place where the meeting would be held.

The delegation and army of the council came to the hall of meetings. The army surrounded the hall and the delegations met. The council members insisted on having the perpetrator of the deed against Salem surrender to the council delegation and army. Maintaining their philosophy, the crafts group refused. They were using arguments covering all the reasons the crafts primes should relent, but they were refused every time.

It should be noted that the council of Nakom was well liked by the crafts primes who often deferred to them in discussions. But the entire meeting between the two delegations was one-sided. The council presented their point-of-view to the crafts delegation and asked them to answer, "Yes." At no time did they ask the crafts delegation what their opinion was, how they thought, or what they wanted in return. This increasing focus in which council failed to give them permission to tell them what they thought increased their frustration. And as with Meshug, it often leads to aggression.

After a meeting that consumed several days, the crafts delegation shouted at them, "Quiet, quiet! We have a question to ask you."

The council fell silent and to their surprise, relented by saying, "What do you want to ask?"

The senior member of the delegation asked, "If we do not provide you with the person who you want, what will you do to us and our representatives that you are holding?"

The council answered quickly. "They shall not be returned to you until you hand over to us the guilty party. We will send our army to search every house and corner of your territory to find the guilty party. This is an irreversible decision."

There was a long pause and the crafts delegation asked the council to withdraw from the room so they might discuss the matter. The council, expecting the crafts delegates to accept their terms, readily withdrew for several days.

The crafts delegation, often a placid group, was angry by the way the council had dealt with them. And as we remind you, anger and frustration yields to aggression. While the council withdrew and relaxed its army, the crafts delegation ordered an immediate strike against the army and delegation of the council. Since the council had made no preparations for such an attack, the smaller army of crafts organisms had the advantage of surprise. On that day, the 8,000 members of the crafts army overwhelmed the 20,000 soldiers of the council army, and most of them were destroyed. The council delegation was sent back to inform the ruling council what the response of the crafts organisms was to their lack of response to their questions.

It is not necessary to provide to you the details of what happened on this nice and peaceful planet. Anger and frustration grew on the ruling council. For the first time in the history of its planet they used aggression. First, the 10 members of the craft delegation they had earlier seized were severely punished. Then they secretly sent an army of 200,000 Prime-Organisms to the crafts territory. The crafts army, greatly outnumbered, changed their methods of fighting to a way of hiding and attacking from the rear. In this way, the smaller crafts army would be able to defend itself against the superior force of the ruling council. The crafts army also was able to manufacture projectiles to keep themselves at a long distance from the council army while attacking.

At the end of the war there were no winners – only losers. 150,000 of the council army ceased living. Many of the remaining army were damaged, but still alive. Close to 25,000 of the crafts army ceased living. But more critical, the entire economical basis of Matohr was destroyed. The planet went through a period of 200 circuits around its mother star in which the culture, infrastructure, and food sources were damaged. To this day, Matohr has never returned to its grand glory and the happiness of its citizens.

The scholars of Shamym attributed the cause of this war to the original attempt to make an image of the council leader in his absence. Based upon this notion, they reached a point in which they paid more attention to the idols and statues representing Avod, and this led to neglecting the common good of the people.

As with the Matohr rebellion, the group of sages representing each planet convened to analyze the cause of the mass slaughtering that resulted in the rebellion. They concluded that by developing a false substitute for their leader Avod, the substitute and the respect it was assigned became as important as Avod, and thus the primes obeyed the false image. They ended their meeting by developing the following rule.

Rule 2:

If a leader is acting in the best interests of his subjects, it is forbidden to substitute a physical symbol of the leader as an image or substitute for the leader. Nor shall there be a substitute in an abstract way. It should not be built, it shall not be used as a substitute for the leader and his demands and laws, nor shall it be obeyed. Only the leader can create and rule on the commands, and if the command is made, the leader must be obeyed.

CHAPTER
EIGHT

The Bagida Insurrection
The War of Disloyalty

Bagida is a planet like Aretz – your planet. It has a diameter of 8,100 miles or over 13,000 kilometers. Its mother star is approximately 100,000,000 million miles or 160,000,000 kilometers away, about the distance of the mother star on Aretz.

Like Aretz, Bagida was formed in its orbit with its axis at a constant 25 degrees from vertical – again almost the same angle as that of Aretz. Bagida rotates around this axis, with a single rotation taking about 26 Aretz hours, giving its day 12 hours of light and 12 hours of darkness. A single rotation about the mother star takes 410 days – longer but like the year on Aretz. Bagida is in a small solar system of six planets – two of them closer to the mother star and three of them further than Bagida. All five of them are significantly unable to support carbon, hydrogen, and oxygen organisms.

Because of the axis tilt, any area of Bagida close to its poles has four seasons: a cold season, a warm season, and two moderate seasons. The areas of Bagida near its equatorial center have warmer seasons with fewer variations in temperature. The surface of Bagida is almost a duplicate of what exists on Aretz and other planets. As with planets that sustained life, the surface developed into solid and liquid forms, randomly dispersed throughout. The solids were made up of minerals of various forms. The liquid was made from a combination of our most plentiful gasses – in your terminology, hydrogen and oxygen, and a compound of carbon and oxygen.

Under the order of El Shadai, our scientists discovered other planets in our solar system and close-in universe where similar development has occurred – a mineral surface with bi-hydrous oxide liquid in large amounts. Another element we have in plentiful amounts is carbon – probably a by-product of the formation period of our planet and the heat emitted by our mother star. Because I ordered these studies, Bagida organisms consider El Shadai their ultimate leader as do every other major planet we have explored.

Life on Bagida took 50,000,000 orbits to develop. It was not surprising that the major organisms of Bagida were part of a variety of life forms ranging from prime organisms at the highest level, followed by "semi-primes." These were organisms that appeared like the primes, but lacked a thinking unit that would be able to bypass instinctual responses and were trained to carry out some tasks including communicate with the Prime-Organisms. I will discuss them later.

The remaining animal based organisms included those who only acted instinctually and could be raised as a source of protein for food, as well as helped the primes in tasks that required labor too difficult for the prime organisms to do.

Our scientists found, as with all planets in our close-in universe, that SWOW principles occurred on Bagida. The prime organisms evolved through SWOW to have a symmetrical body development, including appendages for locomotion (not unlike those on Aretz) as the gravitational force to enable movement is like that of Aretz. The manipulative appendages also are like those of Aretz, with the upper arms containing muscles for lifting and the lower appendages providing fine abilities through opposing digits.

Because of its size, gravitation pull, and distance from the mother sun, the mixture of atmosphere of Bagida was like that of Aretz – nitrogen, oxygen, and bi-carbon oxide. Indeed, members of our exploration team included prime organisms from Bagida and they interacted with organisms on your planet early in the development of Aretz to learn and understand your civilizations. We will explain this later in this communication.

But first we will describe what happened to Bagida.

Like other planets, Bagidan life started in the water. As the planet cooled, mountains and landmasses replaced the waters due to catastrophic upheavals as the hot center of the planet burst through the outer shell of Bagida. Organisms that had long depended upon living in the water and filtering their oxygen intake through gills, carefully and slowly adopted the gaseous version of oxygen that was found on the landmasses. The SWOW method of change was a good example of how the process of change occurred.

Over millions of orbits, the need for gills became minor and they grew to be vestigial. In later years, the leftover location of gills was found on the faces of the Bagida primes and they were used as an optional organ to gather additional oxygen when needed. Bagidans became fine space travelers. If they landed on a planet that had a lower percent of oxygen than Bagida, they were more likely to survive because of the gill-based addition they could breathe in.

"In Aretz, there are no visible signs of gills on the human body, but we do have other vestigial body parts – tonsils, appendix's, foot anomalies suggesting web feet, etc."

Prime organisms of Bagida had a plentiful supply of protein by consuming the lower organisms. As I mentioned previously, our scientists have found that when prime organisms have this large supply, the growth of the brain is accelerated. Planets that have the most primes who have gained scientific control of the planet and their environment can be traced to high levels of protein. This enables them to manipulate their fine objects and their large objects.

"In Aretz, similar developments have occurred – the SWOW development of our digits, arms and torso, and legs. [Here I am using your term, SWOW, rather than our term, Evolution of the species by natural selection.]"

In Bagida, the SWOW process developed various organisms that were not common on other planets. One organism that was unique was the "semi-prime" organism, about the size of the primes but without their thinking ability. They were trained by the primes. In effect, this class of organisms interacted with the prime organisms by carrying out the tasks needed to help them, but they were passive, did not have the ability to think ahead or create changes in the environment, and were docile by training. They lived with the family units of the prime organisms. The primes treated them very well and their brain could not consider not working for their masters. In our visits to Aretz, we found similar organisms but in a different form – small furry organisms living within the family unit and doing minor chores.

The methods of reproduction among Bagidans were similar to that of Aretz. There were two types of prime organisms: providers and birthers. The providers inseminated the birthers in a pleasurable act. This act introduced half of the genetic materials that was theirs into a sack of the birthers. This then combined with the genetic material supplied by the birthers. The resulting prime organism that developed in the birther's sac was made up of half of the contribution of each pair. The combination of the two sources of genetic material enabled strong lines of newborn Prime-Organisms that joined together.

The Bagida primes were very advanced in brain development. Unlike other planets we have explored, they did not appoint a hierarchy of rulers. Rather, they used their brainpower to go beyond the physical world to a spiritual level. Whereas other planets concentrate on relationships between organisms, the Bagidan prime went beyond their own species. They developed relationships with the beauty of their planet, the colors of the sky, and the shape and colors of the vegetation. In effect, these stimuli provided their advanced brain to obtain satisfaction with inanimate objects and gave them pleasure as an end rather than a means.

As the advanced brains of the primes explored the beauty of their universe, they developed a philosophy seeking to understand why their planet was created, how were the experiences they shared developed, and what could they do to better understand why they and their world existed.

There was a group of primes, more advanced than the others, who came up with a concept that the world they lived in, and the worlds they saw in the dark sky, must have been placed there for a purpose. This led them to envision a supreme force, greater that El Shadai, and greater than their imagination could define.

The Bagida primes spent much time trying to understand the nature of the supreme force. Was it a force that was formed from the original creation of the universe and was still reflected by movements now seen the present universe? Was it a natural sequence in the present universe? Was it a supernatural being creating and controlling what was going on in the present, or was it a random sequence? Whatever the answers were to these theories, the Bagida primes had an overarching issue; why was the universe and the organisms it created and for what purpose?

Since the Bagida culture was a happy one, and the experiences of Bagidan life were pleasant, it came to be believed that to survive, the Begidan society must be free of selfishness and aggression. The society must cherish the use of the thinking unit (or brain as you call it) to understand the world and others in the world.

It must use various modes of thinking without making a preference for those who think in detail versus those who think in broad concepts. When a prime organism makes a judgement of others, it uses two instincts: understanding and tolerance or discipline and punishment. When considering some aesthetic stimuli of the universe, it should recognize two alternatives: those who cherish its beauty or those who cherish its functionality. When they complete a task, it chooses two instincts: preferring triumph over others or accepting satisfaction by doing well.

Many thinkers and seekers among the Bagida prime organisms came to this theory and developed a belief system that gave credit to a Supreme Force. They formed small groups and societies that met and related to this invisible force by song, dance, and poetry. As El Shadai, I was pleased with the thinking of the Begidan organism. It showed a strong philosophy of peaceful living.

However, Bagidans, while understanding the concept of the Supreme Force, could not fully comprehend it. Bagidans lived in a beautiful forest, which in warmer zones of the planet became a jungle. There were many lower forms of life in this environment and they did not believe that they should destroy these lower forms. The leaders of the society found that in certain areas of the planet, the Prime-Organisms in the environment were using these lower forms as food, and through this diet were provided with high quality protein. They found that those primes who were consuming proteins grew larger thinking units and began to use high levels of understanding and learning.

There were disagreements about using the lower level organisms as food, especially the semi-primes. For some parts of the planet, it was forbidden for them to eat other life forms and it was preferred to consume growths and food that came from plant life. Some Bagidan philosophers ruled that the fruits of trees and plants should be used for food, and the fruits of living beings not be used at all.

Over time, the success and value of the protein eaters began to become superior. Their thinking units led them to have a greater hold over the other primes. This phenomenon took over, and within 5,000 Begidan years the protein eating population became one of the strongest and smartest of the entire close-in planets.

With this unstoppable growth of their minds, and within thousands of Bagidan years, the Bagidan primes worked together to understand the nature of the Supreme Force. Groups of their smartest argued. What could the nature of the Supreme Force be? What must the primes do in growing the society? What shall the morals of the Bagidan population be? How will Bagidans interact among themselves? What would the Supreme Force expect of them? They published large tomes of their arguments and conclusions. They broke down the functions of primes and developed a set of rules within which major interactions of Begidans were carried out: family relationships, judging others, treatment of children, loyalty to partners, rules of work, rules for treating each other, rules of treating primes with which you have opposite opinions, gathering together with similar thinking primes, how to communicate with the Supreme Force, rules for reproducing new primes, etc. There were many "schools" of primes and they had to relate to each other in a proper way.

"The process you are describing is like that which I learned when I was young. My history showed that 2,000 years before we met (in the year 2014), the people I came from went through a stage of understanding the supreme force, which we called God. The history on Aretz resulted in wars, hatred, and control that are still being fought out in Aretz. El Shadai had a small comment that he spoke to me":

"You will be with me for my visit and you will see that stage in history."

"I was amazed to hear that remark. I could never imagine that my journey would take me there."

As the Bagidan populations of the various groups and societies grew, there was a strong morality that filled the planet and its inhabitants. Over time, the rules of dealing with the Supreme Force started to recede into the background and were not threatened. But as these rules receded, new prime organisms attempted to expand the teachings of the Supreme Force beyond what was accepted. Two such instances occurred with serious consequences.

Some of the group leaders believed that they were related to the Supreme Being, El Shadai himself, and therefore, as offspring, their group deserved greater power than other groups. Some of these leaders became "demi-beings" – a live representation of the Supreme Being. This, of course, went against the rule of *not* taking the place of the Supreme Being.

Other groups had leaders who chose to teach and interpret the rules of the Supreme Being. They claimed a direct line from the origin of the beliefs of the Supreme Being and refused to accept those who claimed they inherited him through birth, and therefore owned the rules passed by other sources.

The main tenet of this Bagidan belief system is that there was a single Supreme Being that led to this society. This was expressed by a rule held close to their people.

"This Supreme Force is a single entity and no one can take its place."

This was expressed three time per day by the prime belief system of Bagidan society. The rule was:

"Hear us Bagidans – The Prime Being, El Shadai, is your guide and he is singular!"

With its outstanding knowledge and its brilliant leadership, Bagida became the leading planet in the close-in universe and its teachings spread out to all other planets.

Two schools of belief were taught to the other planets.

One was based upon the leaders being part of the physical line of Supreme Being and in effect being the offspring of the Supreme Being.

The other school was based upon the teaching and interpretation of the moral rules of the Supreme Being. Their teachings grew from their thinking and interpretations of the concept of the Supreme Being.

As time passed and the population of Bagida grew, their methods of explaining their philosophies to the other planets in the close-in universe were systematized. There were many arguments and disagreements between these two schools of belief.

Those who claimed to be direct descendants of the Supreme Being – "*The Descendants*" – convinced their students that because they were the offspring of the Force, they had powers that were like the Supreme Being.

In contrast, the school based upon teaching and interpretations could bring into the belief system of the Supreme Being the use of the thinking organs in their head. They were named "*The*

Knowledgeable." The resulting set of belief systems developed into a more inclusive and less totalitarian organization of beliefs.

These two groups developed two separate societies to govern their followers. The Descendants developed a top to down governing force based upon the claim of the leaders that they emerged from a personal relationship to the Supreme Force.

On the other hand, the Knowledgeables developed a society that was based on the interpretive theories and merit of their leadership and scholars. The society was formed as a meritocracy where those who became leaders were those that had the most knowledge in teaching and interpreting their beliefs in the Supreme Force. *"My history suggests that Aretz experienced the same division. It did not happen without many lives lost."*

In the beginning of the belief of the Supreme Being, the two societies competed with the other to teach the other organisms the meaning of the Supreme Being. While they competed, there was a friendly competition and they respected each other.

The Rift of the Societies

About 400 Bagidan years after the creation of the two societies, there came a leader of the Descendants who wished to gain control over the Knowledgeables and gain preference for his group among the prime organisms. His name was ***Con-Stan-Tian***. He believed that the Descendants should become the leaders in teaching the meaning of the Supreme Force. That meant that the philosophy of the Descendants should become the only source of interpretation on the role of the Supreme Force and its relationship with the prime organisms in the close-in universe.

The leaders of the Knowledgeable, by their nature, were passive and avoided aggression. They concentrated on learning and interpreting what they considered to be the nature of the Supreme Being. They believed that the thinking unit of the prime organism is what makes it different from the lower organisms.

However, they were shocked when the leaders of the Descendants attacked their group to make the principles of the Descendants the prime advantage over the Knowledgeable. Never were the beliefs in the Supreme Being questioned.

After 400 years, the Descendants had become the larger of the two schools of study, and they were followed by much more of the population than the Knowledgeable. They owed their success by the appeal to others as them being the direct offspring of the Supreme Being. This belief was taken as fact and reinforced by the leaders of the Descendants. Con-Stan-Tian, a creative leader, sought a physical proof of the Descendants' connection to the Supreme Force. During a trip while researching and teaching the history of the Descendants, he found a bone that came from an unknown source.

He used the bone as a symbol that he attributed to the initial offspring of the Supreme Being. Because of this physical evidence, many followers of the Supreme Force became followers of the Descendants. They wore amulets in the shape of the bone and even designed the entrances to their homes in a similar way to how the bone was shaped.

"At this stage, I have come to believe that the Bagida experience may have inspired the future history of Aretz. Con-Stan-Tian sounds much like the Emperor, Constantine, whose mother found the wooden cross and shroud of the "Son of God.""

The leaders of the Descendants were anxious to degrade the work of the Knowledgeable by preventing them from practicing their study and discussion to define the Supreme Being. Allies of the Descendants sought to punish the Knowledgeable by interrupting their dialogues, eliminating the safe environment for them, and in some cases, striking them with stones and cutting implements. In one community on Bagida, the senior ruling group of the Knowledgeable was rounded up and thrown off a high parapet that ended the lives of these leaders. Being a passive group, the Knowledgeable hid their meetings or moved them to secret places. The impact of this move was that the Descendants became the major source of information about the Supreme Force while the Knowledgeable were curtailed from communicating their beliefs.

Over the centuries, after the uprising against the Knowledgeables, they had found a movement promoting a specific area of the planet where they could settle into and defend themselves without punishment or exile by the Descendants. Since their behavior grew in many years of continuous study, wherein knowledge became a meritocracy, the SWOW principle enabled them to concentrate on using their wisdom that had grown over the years to study the sciences of physics, biology, and theories of weapons for their protection. Two thousand years after the division of the Descendants and the Knowledgeable, the latter group sought revenge for the mishandling of their learned leaders by the Descendants. They developed a strong army based upon scientific findings involving advances in the splitting of the uranium atom, which was accompanied by a major explosion covering a wide area. They gathered their weapons in hidden locations and attacked the leadership of the Descendants. Millions of the Descendants were evaporated through these weapons and the Knowledgeable, despite their freedom from the Descendants, were struck with regret – an emotion that was an outgrowth of study, where the use of alternative decisions was respected.

El Shadai was truly upset by this action. Using all the power he could command, he forced the remaining Knowledgeable to realize that their action was counter to the rules of the close-in universe and those of the Supreme Being. They immediately made amends to their former enemy and created a law so that these evil destructive behaviors would not happen again. Since the wars with the Descendants considered the Supreme Being one that they specifically owned by descent, a rule was created that forbid claims of direct descent as a way of exerting power.

Rule 3:

You shall not take the belief of the Supreme Force and its Power in vain, for the Supreme Force will not hold guiltless those who take His name and existence in vain.

Hear Oh Bagidans! The Supreme Force is the only Force from which all knowledge emanates.

CHAPTER
NINE

The Aiphot Crisis
The War of the Fatigued

The planet Aiphot is unique in our universe. It is 30,000 miles in diameter, which gives it a heavy gravitational pull. But it is located close enough to its mother star to have a temperate climate. The result of these two factors is that the SWOW process has resulted in prime organisms being extremely strong. Their propulsion units (legs) are large and muscular, and the manipulation organs (hand and arms) are strongly developed and practiced in the use of tools and manipulation of objects that could be used in games and competition.

Since the prime organisms on Aiphot use strength and manipulation as central to the interaction of the society, brain development was not critical, even to the extent that the brain was smaller than most of its neighboring planets. Our scientists have found that brain development is best related to organisms that must think of numerous ways to manipulate their environment. Since the primes of Aiphot manipulated better that any of the sub-Prime-Organisms on the planet, their superiority was gained by physical power, and not thinking. Thus, Aiphot primes had fewer sub-primes that they could control and train and use in helping them fulfill their tasks.

Every planet in our close-in universe must develop its own method of supporting its population and gathering materials for ingestion, trading, and providing meaningful labor for its population. Many of these tasks are done under the sponsorship of other planets (much like the building tasks of Matohr.) Our planet, Shamym, provided tasks to be done by Aiphot. After many revolutions of the planet around its mother star, the tasks given to Aiphot included lifting heavy objects, building large edifices, operating heavy tools used in building, and manufacturing heavy objects. The tasks for these types of work were commonly done on smaller size planets where the muscle and mobility of Aiphot workers were respected, as they had superior strength than that of the organisms on the planets that used them. The primes of Aiphot found their efforts in strength and motion simple on planets with smaller size and gravity.

Over several eons, the primes of Aiphot expanded their capabilities to many other functions. One such function was the resolution of conflicts on other planets. We have discussed the negative impact that frustration has on aggression. Frustration arose from many sources. Sometimes the frustrated primes of a planet acted against their offspring, and their close-in society. In those situations, the rulers of the planets that hired them needed to have a group to maintain civil order, especially at time of unhappiness due to shortages of food. The strength and mobility of the Aiphot primes were suited to these tasks which led them to create, train, and practice with weapons to keep order.

The Aiphot primes had much demand for their services. The population of the planet had thriving businesses and commercial relations with other planets. The providers on Aiphot trained and spent long periods of time on other planets carrying out their functions. In return, they were paid in food and shelter materials. The birthers on the planet remained on the surface, raising and training their offspring.

Over several eons, the Aiphot society found that it was necessary to have an organization to identify, train, and raise large numbers of its citizen to send them to planets it served. They were aware that El Shadai was the leader of the nearby solar system and universe. Aiphot organisms realized they needed strong and intelligent leaders and leader council to supervise and organize its workers to serve over 350 close-in planets in an efficient way. El Shadai helped to advise the leaders of the planet how to organize Aiphot. The leader group helped them because planning and organization was beyond the natural intelligence of the citizens.

Since the management and training of the hired workforce required a great deal of knowledge, the decision was made that a strong leader would have the sole decision of managing and controlling the work groups. The leader and his council were selected by merit. When the first leader and council were formed, calls went out to the primes of Aiphot to apply for the leader's position. The contest was made up of several parts: general knowledge of leadership, understanding of motivations and needs of the workers, talents in understanding which organisms excelled in specific work areas, and ability to organize work groups to have compatibility within the group. Out of a final group of 5,000 candidates who were tested, 30 were selected as the top performers. The highest performer I chose was named **Hachma**. He out-performed the remaining 29 primes, who were made the members of his council. Over time, when the council and leaders grew old and weak, new primes who had qualified for leadership in the same means and merits as the original leader replaced them. The new leader was named **Hachma-2** – a separate digit counting the order of rule differentiated each one.

A second call went out to the 350 close-in planets they served for each to select an expert on their behalf to advise Hachma-2 and his council on the work and tasks they would be doing for them. This was recognition that even the best of Aiphot prime organisms may not be the brightest in the universe. These advisers would provide information and consultation about the risks, the population needs, and the physical challenges faced by the organisms of Aiphot working for each planet. This group would be a board of consultants for Hachma-2 and his council.

Within the close-in universe, the exploits of the Aiphot workers became legendary. They built the mighty cities and domes on Shamym. They built the buildings and structures of Kokav. They maintained the operation of the interplanetary vehicles of Zalzul. They set up and moved the heavy artistic output of Matohr. And most importantly, they maintained civil order on countless other planets.

For reasons we have already hinted about, civil order became a key need among the prime societies in the close-in universe. In effect, they became a professional army. This was especially so for those societies in which providers and birthers attempted to live with their families in monogamous groupings with their offspring. These societies tend to breed competitive instincts between families, partners, and siblings. Coming from a peaceful planet like Shamym, it became strange for us to understand and observe how primes that should be close to each other tended to have the greatest degree of conflict. Since many of the close-in planets of our universe have developed in this way, the strong primes of Aiphot were often called upon to reduce the conflicts and restore order when these clashes emerged.

Aiphot developed a major crisis by using its primes in the aid of other planets. About 1,000,000 of its primes were hired and trained as police to keep order on the other planets. About 675,000 were trained to do construction on the other planets. Another group of 1,200,000 primes were hired and trained in moving heavy materials so that the proficient builders and construction primes could do the skilled task of building. The income generated by these 2,875,000 Aiphot workers was needed to earn funds and foods necessary to feed their families and the Aiphot population.

The crisis faced by Hachma-2 was caused by population figures and the need to send to send trained workers to the close-in universe. Unfortunately, the population of Aiphot was limited to providing no more than 3,000,000 workers. But demand for its various services require more than the 3,000,000 primes. Hachma-2 and his advisory council explored how they could increase the work required to support the planet.

The advisory council calculated that since the average day in which Aiphot rotates is the earth equivalent of 42 hours, they had 126,000,000 hours of potential work that could be done. However, the primes of Aiphot required 13 hours per day of rest to renew the thinking organs. This translated to 39,000,000 hours. Hachma-2 suggested that if rest were limited to seven hours per day, they could gain 18,000,000 hours of labor, or the equivalent of adding approximately 428,000 additional laborers. The council met and Hachma-2, who was elected because he was the smartest of the group, convinced them to enact this new rule. Without testing it, they calculated that the workforce would be increased by 14 percent without having to find, test, and train more workers.

The time and task schedules were recalculated based upon these additional hours available. It was decided that the extra tasks to be filled would be those that required interactions with local primes, rather than those that required work and building tasks. These were mostly those tasks that required discipline and keeping order on the client planets.

Matohr was a planet that had hired them as a police force to keep order and help in the assignments or work schedules, along with the enforcement of the schedules. The task required them to ensure that the artistic community of the planet was able to handle the workload and complete the job assigned to them.

One group of 250 artists was assigned to a troop of 10 Aiphot supervisors. Since artists were more passive and less aggressive, this was a simple task for them to fulfill. The Aiphot contractors worked every day and found their Matohr charges to be an easy group to supervise. The troop, like all Aiphot contractors, agreed to work the new shifts that Hachma-2 developed – 35 hours of work and seven hours of rest. Since the idea of 10 supervisors assigned to 250 artists appeared to be successful, Hachma-2 made this approach universal, both on Matohr and all other planets using Aiphot workers.

However, lack of rest started to have an impact on the thinking and temperaments of the Aiphot workers who were prime organisms.

With their bodies overcome by fatigue, a war broke to overthrow the forced work schedules. It was found that with fatigue, logic and thinking is diminished, and relationships are compromised. Local insurrections by the citizens of Aiphot caused them to revolt, but the superior strength and strategy of the Aiphot workers overcame the revolt. Almost four million Matohr citizens died in this war. After the carnage, it was agreed that the fault lied with the rulers of the planet. They permitted the development of a philosophy to increase productivity by forcing their army and workers to devote a tremendous amount of time to doing duties for the government by having to work with very little rest. The impact of working without rest led be errors and mistakes.

This war and its destruction led to a new rule of guidance:

Rule 4:

Enable a single day – the seventh day – a Sabbath Day for rest and rejuvenation. Use it to learn new tasks and activities, relate to other organisms, share the love of your environment, and plan for the next week. Also use it to meet and enjoy the prime organisms in your family unit and provide your thinking unit with a chance to recycle.

CHAPTER
TEN

The Kokav - Zalzul War
The War of the Revengeful Son

For over 1,000 of our orbits, Kokav and Zalzul had developed stable methods for the organization of each of their civilizations and the interactions of its primes. I will tell you about these two planets and how they came to be enemies of each other. This transformation from friends to enemies led to countless deaths on both planets and on Shamym.

Kokav

Kokav was a planet of approximately 7,800 miles (12,400 km.) in diameter. It was situated at a distance from its mother star that provides it with a temperate climate that varied by orbit position from 100 to 0 degrees Fahrenheit (38 to -18 degrees Celsius). With a diameter similar to that of your planet, enabling it to hold an oxygen rich atmosphere, along with the temperature variation indicated, it would have been a hospitable home for citizens of your planet.

The three pairs of symmetrical organs, for locomotion, manipulation, and the three linked factors of emotion – directing and thinking – Kokav Prime-Organisms developed in a similar manner as with your planet, but with minor variations. For example, because of shallow water coverage on Kokav, the feet of the Prime-Organisms were webbed. This enabled them to survive predators in the shallow water. Those that did so, through the SWOW mechanism, passed their webbed feet to future generations. Because of plentiful protein from the lower organisms, which included the water based organisms and land based organisms, the brain development of the Kokav primes was excellent. Because of these factors, Kokavites found that the use of science, technology, and travel became the prime functions of the planet.

Kokav was a planet on which providers and birthers accomplished their reproduction in a way that was pleasurable to both. They brought up their young organism for the first seven orbits of their life, prior to their being given over to the EEMA system for training, screening, and assignment. What violence arose in Kokav were those actions that were related to the chemicals secreted in the emotional section of the thinking unit when providers and birthers met other providers and birthers. Since the pleasure of reproduction was unique and could not be clearly communicated to others, curiosity grew about how the pleasure would be with another birther and/or provider. It was not uncommon for Kokav providers to mate with other birthers and in some cases, attempt to mate with other providers. Birthers, too, attempted to mate with other birthers. What was discovered during these years of experimentation was that the pleasure between same pair organisms (provider/provider and birther/birther) could be attained, but without reproduction.

Though apparently, the normal process of reproduction encouraged the growth of affinity between the couples and their offspring. When this affinity was interfered with, chemical secretions in the thinking unit produced an emotion akin to what your planet would call "jealousy." It was found that the dysfunction of the emotion aspects of the Prime-Organisms interfered with the linked factors of planning and thinking. Organisms were no longer able to function in their assigned tasks. Such Prime-Organisms were assigned to less productive tasks that required little planning and thinking. Since this reassignment was not helpful to the society, the leadership group of Kokav made provider and birther activities outside of the original unit illegal.

When I was asked, El Shadai helped Kokav organize itself under a single leader who oversaw all the functions of the planet to plan and assign tasks to its Prime-Organisms. Under this Supreme Leader were 10 organizations: food and sustenance, training and education, homes and dwellings, and locomotion. This was done in an organized process with organisms assigned to specific functions after their maturity and education.

Approximately 400 of our orbits ago, Kokav was a friend of Shamym and we traded with them freely. Since Kokav used power to propel their space vehicles and manufacture their goods, they required energy-processed gold as a power source. The processing was done by a processor planet – a planet on which the entire population was on a level of organism development, as a result of the SWOW process, in which the lower intelligence of its Prime-Organisms precluded their abilities to utilize and advance tasks such as invention, science, interplanetary travel, and understanding of societal interactions and morals. Zalzul is a processor planet.

Zalzul

Zalzul was a planet of approximately 13,000 miles (21,000 km) in diameter. It was situated at a distance from its mother star that provided it with a climate that varied by orbit position from +40 to -40 degrees Fahrenheit (+4 to -40 degrees Celsius). Its diameter provided a strong gravitational pull resulting in an oxygen rich atmosphere concentrated closer to the surface of the planet. During diplomatic and trading visits to Zalzul, Kokavites required clothing that kept their body temperature warm, and their travel was aided by devices that compensated for their lack of locomotion due to the heavier gravity.

As to the three pairs of symmetrical organs – for locomotion, manipulation, and thinking and monitoring – Zalzul Prime-Organisms developed in unique ways driven by the SWOW principle. Their legs were twice the thickness as those on Kokav and your planet.

Their manipulative organs were also thicker in the parts that were closest to the torso so that they could lift the heavier apparatus needed for personal use as well as for use in their factories. The extremities of their arms used for finer manipulation were thin, almost belying the volume of their arms. We believe that the SWOW principle favored those on Zalzul who were able to do fine manipulation.

Finally, the nature of their environment may have impacted the development of the unit that controls emotion, directing, and thinking. Their thinking units were not as well developed as those residents of Kokav. We believe that this was due to a function of the diameter and temperature of Zalzul. Those that were able to survive in Zalzul were those whose primary motivation for survival was to seek and hold shelter from the weather, especially the cold winds that buffer the planet. The average range of travel of those that survived was much smaller than those who lived on Kokav and Shamym. This limited range of travel favored those who limited their range of stimuli. The lack of a wide range of stimuli reduced the volume of their thinking unit so that they were not curious about their environment. The result was a lack of science, travel, and complex thought and emotion.

Similarly, there was paucity of lower life forms and living organisms. So while Kokav, Shamym, and your planet had plentiful protein from lower organisms, there was less brain development of the Zalzul primes. Because of these factors, Zalzulites concentrated their planets activities on lower forms of manufacturing that were capable of being accomplished by the specification, direction, and wishes of others.

Finally, because of the temperature extremes, Zalzulites developed (through SWOW) with a hairy and fur-filled body. When contacting other planets, including Kokav and Shamym, Zalzul recognized that their bodies, with large legs, big arms, and hairy skin, was not pleasing to the eyes of others. Our scientists believe that the preference for simple shapes and smooth skin is a basic instinct of all life forms on the universe.

Like Kokav, Zalzul was a planet on which providers and birthers accomplished their reproduction in a way that was pleasurable to both. They brought up their young organisms for the first eight orbits of their life, prior to them being given over to the EEMA system for training, screening, and assignment. As with Kokav, violence arose in Zalzul when actions that were related to the chemicals secreted in the emotional section of the thinking unit erupted when providers and birthers met other providers and birthers. The pleasure of reproduction was unique and could not be clearly communicated to others. Curiosity grew about how the pleasure would be with another birther and/or provider. It was not uncommon for Zalzul providers to mate with both birthers and with other providers. Birthers, too, attempted to mate with other birthers. And just like on Kokav, they discovered during these years of experimentation that the pleasure between same pair organisms (provider/provider and birther/birther) could be pleasurable, but without reproduction.

As we have seen with Kokav, the normal process of reproduction in Zalzul encouraged the growth of affinity between the couples and their offspring, setting off chemical secretions in the thinking unit that produced an emotion akin to "jealousy." It was found that the dysfunction of the emotion aspects of the Prime-Organisms interfered with the linked factors of planning and thinking. Organisms would no longer be able to function in their assigned tasks. Such Prime-Organisms were assigned to less productive tasks that required little planning and thinking. But although these dysfunctions were not helpful to the society, Zalzul leaders and its population had a more primitive emotional development. The leadership group of Zalzul made provider and birther activities acceptable and legal, but did not punish crimes of jealousy, including murder.

Zalzul, being a planet that served the needs of other planets, structured itself under a single leadership organization that oversaw all of the functions of the planet to plan and assign tasks to its Prime-Organisms. Under this Supreme Leader were three organizations: food and sustenance, homes and dwellings, locomotion and production. This was done by ruler fiat, with organisms assigned to specific tasks as they reached an age at which they could contribute to the society.

The Conflict

As I previously indicated, Shamym had the largest supply of gold in the universe. Our scientists developed a method of processing gold and changing it to a source of power. One way of deriving energy is by the power of the light of a mother sun. For many orbits of time, this ability was found to have high inefficiencies. It was not because the light was inadequate, but rather because most of the light coming to their energy sensors was not being absorbed.

They discovered that metals like gold, silver, and platinum had the ability to absorb the energy more efficiently by changing their surfaces to have millions of microscopic vertical cones so that the light entering it was completely absorbed. This enabled us to draw energy from even the most distant light sources to maintain trajectories and feed our heavy power needs when we were closer to a bright light source, such as a sun or even reflected from a nearby planet.

To enable the gold to absorb distant light, raw gold was modified by the Zalzul factories. It was made into flat continuous strips, upon which lasers cut beams of light, cone shaped channels. Zalzul provided these to Kokav and they were used for all the power necessary for the functioning of the planet, its scientific research and development, and its travel to faraway worlds and galaxies. Most importantly, Kokav shared their abilities with Shamym, and this became a key factor in the development of its science and travel.

At the time of the Great War, **P'ari** claimed that he was the leader of Zalzul. In fact, his father, **Pr'am**, was the true leader. El Shadai knew Pr'am and we worked together. I advised him on his work tasks. His son, P'ari, believed that his father did not keep up with the younger people. P'ari belittled his father and his rule in the eyes and thinking of his population. Eventually, the population of Zalzul no longer accepted Pr'am as a leader and his son, a younger more vibrant organism, wrested control of the planet. P'ari was a large strong prime organism with a thick coat of dark fur. In the early stages of the economic exchange development with Kokav, he had convinced his father that he should be the leader to discuss the commercial treaties with Kokav. Since Pr'am was reaching the end part of his life, he thought that P'ari should take over his responsibilities temporarily before a new leader was chosen. P'ari visited Kokav many times to discuss and agree upon the treaties of trade. These discussions were between P'ari and his experts, and **Mene**, my self-appointed leader of Kokav.

In his trips to Kokav, P'ari was introduced to Mene's birther, **Hel'n**. P'ari stared at Hel'n for a long time to the extent that his attention was noticeable to Mene and Hel'n. As he gazed at her, he was struck with her perfect symmetry. Her exoskeleton skin covering was smooth and unblemished, her feet were perfectly webbed, the shape of her torso was flawless, and she appeared to be as smart as the providers, despite that she lived the role of a birther.

Since P'ari knew that without the ability of Zalzul to produce the gold energy sources for Kokav, the Prime-Organisms of Kokav would be unable to run their planet. His mind hatched a plot based upon the secretions that produce jealousy and rage.

He told Mene that on behalf of Zalzul he would agree to the terms of the treaty, but he wanted Hel'n to conduct the final agreement on Zalzul. His excuse was that the organisms of Zalzul needed to trust the agreement with his treaty and that Hel'n would be the organism that would sign for Kokav. Mene agreed, because he was a gentle ruler with no experience in plotting, jealousy, or rage.

One orbit later in time, dressed in gravity suits and thick warm covers, Hel'n and her retinue of aides transferred to Zalzul to execute the final agreement. Upon the arrival of the retinue, P'ari had the entire group captured and detained. He told Hel'n that the treaty would not be approved unless Mene let him have her as his own birther. These demands were communicated to Kokav.

Mene received this message and was upset by its content. Hel'n had been his birther for five times. Mene and Hel'n developed a bond cemented by their five offspring. In all his dealings with Zalzul in the past, Pr'am had been a trustworthy partner. Now his son was the leader and all the agreements they had negotiated were threatened, as well as the companionship of Hel'n and the lives of those organisms in her retinue.

Mene sent back a message refusing the offer. He pointed out that providers from Kokav and birthers from Zalzul could not produce an organism that properly belonged in either planet. He reiterated that Hel'n was on a diplomatic mission and she was his birther.

The return message from P'ari was grim and angry. An automatonic ship was dispatched from Zalzul to Kokav using the fastest black hole path to return. In it was the following message from P'ari:

"I wish not to have Hel'n for purposes of birthing. She is to become my object of pleasure for as long as I wish to use her. You must accept my offer or I will take strong action against Kokav. I will stop producing the gold power sources, and I will increase the value for Kokav to receive these power sources. I wish an immediate answer to my demand."

In the hold of the ship were the mutilated bodies of ten of the aides in the retinue.

Mene experienced emotions that he had never experienced before. The rights of relationships between providers and birthers were a basic rule in Kokav. Because of these strictures, Kokavites had never developed ways of dealing with them or the emotions that accompany them. To help him deal with this issue, Mene called a meeting of the ruling council.

The ruling council was a group of advisors that were selected as the brightest Prime-Organisms on the planet. Each one was an expert in a certain field of science: physical, astrophysical, mathematical, biological, economic, psychic, nano-technological, and interspecies psychic thought.

He explained the situation to the council advisors. He reiterated the closeness he had with Hel'n and the result if he ignored the demand, the tragic loss of the ten retinue members (each a trusted advisor and expert in interplanetary trade), the remaining aides that were part of the retinue that were still alive, the economic threat to Kokav from a lack of gold power sources, and the penalty to the entire planet if they angered P'ari.

His council discussed the issue in depth. Most of the council members believed that if Mene were to reject the request, there was a likely chance that all would be lost – Hel'n, the remaining retinue members, and of lesser concern, the entire economic relationship between Kokav and Zalzul. Mene did not think that P'ari would negotiate unless he could achieve his main goal, the use of Hel'n as a source of selfish pleasure. However, if he "gave" P'ari what he desired, he might be able to have him agree to several requests that would enable Kokav to have some time to develop a counter strategy. What this strategy would be was still an issue to be resolved, but the Kokav council, working together, would be able to develop it. Even this decision was difficult to Mene, for as Kokav stalled for time, P'ari would defile Hel'n. He knew that the weight of rule would require him to ignore his own personal needs for the good of the planet he ruled.

The council agreed that initially they needed to have intelligence on Zalzul to communicate both with Hel'n and the retinue, as well as to know what P'ari was planning. The council expert on nano-technological science offered a solution.

They had developed tiny molecules that were programmed to combine with other specialized molecules. In joining together, they would become larger sized organisms. Since they were molecular, the larger sized organism could, in and of itself, be microscopic with the ability to combine and perform its specified function and then break apart. The time of this process was measured as 15 nanoseconds.

The plan that was developed was that on one of the missions to Zalzul for exchanging raw gold for processed fuel, the transfer vehicle would be full of these molecular nano-particles. While the vehicle was in orbit, the different groups of molecules would move, invisibly, to the surface of Zalzul. One group would be designed to communicate messages to the prisoners. Other particles would be programmed to turn into laser weapons and fulfill other tasks. An experimental group of molecules would be programmed to enter the thinking units of the enemies to understand their plans and impact on their attention and thought processes. These molecules analyzed the secretions of an organism's thinking units and modified the secretions to impact memory, aggression, and emotion.

So the message went out to P'ari that he could have Hel'n if he pledged to conserve the lives of the retinue members and continue the production of the processed gold power source. P'ari agreed to this offer, dictating higher prices for the processed gold. He gave Kokav a deadline of time to accept these terms, equal to 1/3 of the orbit of Zalzul. When the message vehicle landed on the planet of Zalzul, a small group of the basic molecules were released into the atmosphere of the planet.

The molecules dispersed over the surface, seeking out the location of P'ari, Hel'n, and the remaining retinue party. Some of the molecules recombined into messaging units, and Hel'n and the retinue were located. Simultaneously the molecules entered the hearing canals of each prisoner and explained that they had been sent by Mene and that an attempt at rescuing them by Kokav would be made as soon as accurate intelligence was gathered and a plan conceived. This would occur when the first gold transfer vehicle arrived. They were told to have patience and keep this information confidential.

When P'ari received the message from Mene in the traditional way of communication, the molecules that specialized in reading thoughts recombined in an area near P'ari. They identified the frequency of his thoughts and gathered them for transfer and analysis that were sent back to Kokav. When these transmissions came back to Mene, the nanotechnology group specializing in thinking signals analyzed them. Mene reconvened his advisory group and told them he was happy to report that P'ari accepted the message and considered the action to be a total victory for him and Zalzul. This gave him the ability to mount the counterattack on Zalzul.

Many revolutions of the planet were used to develop the strategy. During this time, word from Zalzul was not good. P'ari, believing that he had won the battle completely, continued to use Hel'n as his concubine. Hel'n often felt that if it weren't for a plan to free the group she would end her life. Mene, a calm and civilized being, developed increasing anger and a feeling of revenge on P'ari. P'ari, believing he had power over Kokav, increased the value and costs of the gold fuel. This made life on Kokav miserable. Travel, comforts, and relationships with other planets had to be curtailed. Kokav's friendly relationship with Shamym was minimized during this period.

However, a plan was developed. It involved a trip to Zalzul for the purpose of bringing the raw gold to be processed into energy sheets. Hidden in the hold of the 17 ships would not be gold, but a highly trained army led by Mene. The army of each ship had

3,000 organisms, brought up to be highly aggressive. The army was equipped with weapons that used the splitting of elemental atoms for power that generated tremendous heat. They would be supported by the nanoparticles that could combine into laser weapons.

The force of 17 ships started their journey to Zalzul. When they came within the outer orbit of Zalzul, the nanoparticles were released. One group of particles communicated their presence and plan to the retinue and Hel'n individually. The second group of particles, which had the laser power, took up positions near the entranceways of each room of the palace of P'ari and his advisors. The third group of molecules had the power to impact the secreted chemicals of thinking organs of P'ari and his advisors. To prevent P'ari from finding out about the hidden army, the nanoparticles that impacted the thinking units of the rulers of Zalzul would confuse the perceptions that were based upon the result of both seeing and hearing. They were also programmed to scan the thinking organs to identify major thoughts, plans, and emotions that were threatening to the mission.

Before the retinue that contained the army and hidden nanoparticles arrived, P'ari was pleased that he had brought Kokav to the state that they were forced to obey his rules. He called for a celebration of his people with special types of food and liquids. Many of the liquids were based upon the minerals of mercury and the liquid of alcohol. P'ari, his advisors, and his army celebrated during the dark portion of their day. Inhibitions were loosened as the mercury compromised the reasoning of the thinking organ and the alcohol reduced the control of inhibitions.

When the light of the mother star came up the next day, P'ari and his armies were attempting to return their bodies and thinking units to normal. Unknown to them, the Kokav nanoparticles had been released and were heading to the planet.

When the light of daybreak reached their eyes, it took great effort to regain their senses. The liquid of alcohol had the impact of reducing their inhibitions. They shouted at each other, the providers tried to have pleasure with the birthers, and the many birthers accepted the entreaties of the providers. They drank copious amounts of alcohol and they never put limits on their inhibitions.

The mercury content of the foods impacted the effect of the alcohol. Their thinking units worked slowly and shortened their memory. Their memory could not maintain a level of inhibition so it could not make decisions that made sense. P'ari himself became aware of how useless his mind had become. At that point in the daybreak, the nanoparticles reached P'ari and his people. However, the nanoparticles were not impacted by the mercury and alcohol consumed. Many of them migrated to the brain of P'ari. He began to notice that he had periods of clear thinking followed by periods of slow uninhibited thought. During one of the periods of clear thinking, he surmised that his brain was being impacted and manipulated by something outside his body. He asked his counsel to explore what was happening to them. Some of his scientists explored whether magnetic forces could have been either a cause or an effect of the thinking changes.

Their experiments suggested that when the magnetic force was close to the thinking units, the alcohol and mercury impacted logical thinking. They found millions of particles on some of the magnets.

It was then that P'ari understood that Kokav had caused this phenomenon. He organized an army and had all of their thinking units demagnetized. They decided to strike against the Kokav expedition. All of the weapons of the Zalzul planet were aimed at the ships of the expedition. In a short time, the expedition party of Kokav was destroyed, evaporated by a nuclear explosion. In total, there were 51,000 soldiers that perished.

In scanning the thoughts of the nanoparticles, the leaders in Kokav received a signal that made no sense. The signal did not respond to them, nor did the leaders of the expedition. There was no signal from the automatic response module in each ship. A series of nanoparticles were parked outside of the orbit of the Kokav ships. The leaders on the planet signaled the nanos to combine into a viewing satellite. The satellite then scanned the orbits of the 17 ships and sent back a picture of a ring of debris in orbit around Zalzul. They concluded that somehow and someway, P'ari found a way to destroy the fleet, even in his drunken state.

In anger and frustration associated with this loss, Mene decided to destroy P'ari and his armies, even at the sacrifice of their hostages. This attack commenced in seven rotations of Kokav and the destruction was successful. P'ari and his army were destroyed and, sadly, Hel'n and the remaining 10 emissaries also perished.

The Council of the Close-in Universe met to determine how to prevent this behavior from happening again. They concluded that since this terrible loss was the result of P'ari overthrowing his father, Pr'am, and his seeking of revenge on those who did not accept his demands, the victorious armies sought a rule that could have prevented this war.

Rule 5:

Show respect and honor to your parents, for their experiences are better than yours for all their lives. Do not overthrow them, harm them, or replace them unless they judge you to be their equal or superior.

CHAPTER
ELEVEN

The Ratzah War of the Murdered Philosopher

Ratzah is a planet of 14,500 kilometers (9,000 miles) in diameter. It is situated 161,000,000 kilometers from its mother star (approximately 100,000,000 miles.) It rotates on an axis parallel to that of its mother star and a single rotation takes approximately 30 hours to complete a single day – 15 hours in light and 15 hours in darkness. It also orbits around its mother star. One single orbit taking 432 days.

We later discovered when we visited your planet, Aretz, that there was a great similarity between Ratzah and Aretz. Because of the comparable similar distances to the mother star, the similar length of the day, and the similar time it takes to rotate around the mother star, the average weather on both planets are similar. The similarity of gravitation pull and temperature enabled both planets to develop an Oxygen rich atmosphere with significant parts of carbon dioxide. The development of the Prime-Organisms, although slightly different from each other, made mutual habitation of both planets possible if needed. A resident of Aretz could live on Ratzah, and vice versa.

Because of the similarity with Aretz, Ratzah organisms developed in a similar way. One celled hydrocarbon organisms associated with the seas of bi-hydrous oxide evolved through the SWOW principal. In the warmest part of Ratzah, those tiny organisms that were able to bond to other similar organisms were most likely to survive. In 35,000,000 rotations around the mother star, more complex organisms developed. Some stayed in the sea, and when others learned to live outside the bi-hydrous oxide environment, they used their propulsion organs from the sea to fly in the air.

A more advanced group of organisms learned to survive on the land – some directly out of the sea, and others from the flying organisms that were on land but had lost the ability to fly. There were differences in body surfaces and make-up that identified their origins. Those that came from the sea had scales on their body surfaces. But once out of the sea, these became vestigial, no longer needed for living on land. Similarly, those that had evolved from flying had small feathers on their body surfaces. Those that lived on land had a body surface made up of fur and/or hair. Over eons, many of these differences were minimized through interbreeding of the various types of organisms.

Prime organisms of both planets used lower organisms as a food source. Some of the organisms were plant-like and used the nourishment of sunlight and carbon dioxide in the atmosphere to sustain themselves. These provided fiber and nutrients to higher organisms.

The more advanced organisms used lesser organisms that lacked intelligence, the ability to manipulate and communicate, and were found in the sea, air and on land. These organisms could be tamed and harvested. The foods they provided were rich in protein, fat, and amino acids. Over much time, this diet enhanced the thinking mechanisms of the prime organisms. When we travelled to Aretz, we found a similar method of developing the characteristics of the prime organisms over there.

Not all aspects of the similarity of the two planets were exact. Since the axis of the rotation is parallel to the mother star (unlike the tilted axis of rotation of Aretz) there were no variations in seasonal weather during the 432-day orbit, nor were there variations on weather along the latitude of Ratzah. The weather of the vertical ends (poles) was always coldest and the temperature of the central horizontal latitude was always warmest. Because of the SWOW principal, there were differences in the color of skin pigment. Those in the colder latitudes had light skin and hair, and those in the warmer latitudes had darker skin and hair.

There were other similarities that made the two societies comparable. Primes decided that the best way for reproduction to take place was with a pair of providers and receivers being in a single relationship. This system evolved when the leaders of the planet discovered that the spiral containing the characteristics of new primes was similar to the spirals of other primes that were their siblings. Being a complex the planet in terms of science and knowledge, providers and receivers within a specific clan knew that most of their offspring would have the same skills and knowledge capacity.

Because of these early decisions, the prime organisms of Ratzah evolved into a highly intelligent group. They were the first in our universe to understand the position and make-up of our close-in universe. They could identify and predict planetary positions. They studied the biological makeup of the Ratzah organisms. They developed space travel mechanisms and discovered wormholes in our universe.

As our close-in universe developed and each planet identified a unique skill that they could offer to the other planets, it became clear that the scientific power of Ratzah was its best offering. Ratzah prime organisms became the scientific consultants of the close-in universe. They categorized the nature of science, its components, and its applications to the rest of the universe.

In order to fulfill these needs, Ratzah developed a need to categorize the scientific functions of their society, train new generations of primes in various functions, and organize the functions in the most efficient ways. In deciding how this should be accomplished, the best and smartest of its population was invited to help organize and develop a way of governing Ratzah.

The following categories were identified:

Organism – The makeup of living organisms and the ways by which they develop and interact.

Elements – The mixture of elements in the universe, how they combine, and how to use them.

Numbers and their Relationships – The use of numbers and the relationship between numbers to explain universal theories and relationships.

Physical Materials – The science of how matter and materials interact, and the universal laws that explain and predict future interactions.

Complex Organism Interactions – The study and understanding of how organisms (at all levels in the development scale) interact in groups and/or environments, and predicting future interactions and environments.

How Organisms Behave – The study and understanding of how individual organisms deal with interactions and stimuli.

Sciences Applied – The study of how all of these sciences come together in real situations.

Sciences of Health – The study and exploration of how organisms on any level can live and exist without illness and disease, and continue to operate in an efficient manner.

"I am amazed that Ratzah could identify various classes of scientific knowledge."

Over time, these categories expanded so that each one became more intricate and were made up of many areas and specialties. To further make these specialties complex, each area of science was often used in other areas. Physics needed mathematics to explore its theories. Health sciences and social sciences used behavioral sciences as applied science in their work.

The prime organisms of Ratzah had developed significant thinking systems. The families were organized in a way so that each offspring of a pair of primes was tested to identify the best scientific area they were most capable of learning and practicing. With great demand for the knowledge and engineering systems offered by Ratzah, the ruling government was presented with the challenge of training its primes. These challenges included educating the young primes, deciding whether the birth process should be guided toward certain skills and areas for the sake of the needs of the society, and identifying scientific and methodological "truths" so that no matter which government or planet Ratzah experts were advising, there would be uniform principles followed. These required the development of standards covering not only scientific principles but also principles impacting the lives and families of the brightest minds of Ratzah.

When I was approached by Ratzah they asked me, El Shadai, to help them organize a ruling class of social, behavioral, and health scientists, chosen by merit, to run the organization and direction of the economy of Ratzah. It was felt that the selection and education of the primes was a critical step in supplying Ratzah with its economy. Over several eras, the population of the planet numbered 26,000,000 Prime-Organisms with an annual growth rate of 3 percent. This meant that in approximately 24 Ratzah years, the population would double. This was considered a rate that was manageable within the resources necessary for space, living conditions, and food.

The ruling class was chosen to be benevolent, with the fulfillment of the planet's needs being a primary goal of those running it. The head of the ruling class that was selected was named **ROSH,** who was a well-renowned philosopher. Rosh was born a birther who had partnered with a provider at a young age. Rosh birthed three Prime-Organisms and was instrumental in their maturation and instruction. Rosh was educated as an expert social scientist. As part of the education and experience of Rosh, it became necessary to learn behavioral science and applied science. Rosh was known on Ratzah as one of the planet's experts on the motivations of prime organisms, as well as on how to evaluate their expertise on their unique subjects and scientific areas. Under the leadership of Rosh and the ruling class, the entire program of education and the decisions on which specialties were needed was made. Rosh was a beloved leader upon whom the entire planet and its economic well-being depended.

Rosh organized the hired workers and specialists of the planet to meet the demands of the close-in universe. These demands were requested and prioritized by requests for a specialist and in guiding the training of the specialists to best meet these needs.

In a typical period of time, Rosh and the ruling class were asked to fill the following demands:

Rakiya needed biological support to create a domed environment for a work area. It also needed behavioral support to train its organisms to work optimally in this environment. It used teams of workers that came from biology, physics, behavioral science, and health sciences.

A disease that weakened their organisms from ingesting and processing oxygen struck **Yakom** beings. They needed specialists in biology, applied sciences, and health scientists to cure the disease and build appropriate oxygen purifying systems to stop the disease.

Zalzul needed help in their purification of gold. They requested consultants in chemistry and physics to increase the purity of the gold they refined for Kokav.

Aiphot identified and tracked a meteor that could have had a chance of impacting the planet. Aiphot requested a team to design a device that would use the power of atomic energy to pulverize the meteor while still distant from Aiphot. Teams of experts in physics, mathematics, and applied sciences developed a safe way to destroy the meteor. The tiny parts of the meteor were burned up in the atmosphere without damaging the planet or its organisms.

There were many other tasks entrusted to them. Several planets needed to develop a means of predicting weather over a long term to help decide when its population could rest and relax when the winds and temperature became moderate. To solve this problem, Rosh combined different teams of unique skills to collaborate to solve these complex issues, coming from areas of physics, biology, chemistry, social sciences, etc.

Although the decisions of Rosh seemed sensible, the experts in each area of science became jealous of one another and thereby angry at other experts. Jealousy was an emotion of which Rosh was unaware. The roots of the jealousy were based upon the sciences.

Some of the sciences were what certain scientists called "hard science" such as chemistry, mathematics, and physics. They were given this nomenclature because studies within them resulted in specific predictable results. A number added to another number always came up with the same results. A gravitational force always resulted in the prediction calculated, and a compound of elements always resulted in the same combination.

Other sciences were called "soft science" such as social sciences, applied sciences, health sciences, behavioral sciences, and medical sciences. They were named this way because, although there were theories and experiments conducted in all these fields, there were no perfect abilities to predict their outcomes. Unlike the "hard" sciences, the personality and proficiency of those who worked in these "soft" sciences governed their ability to clearly emerge with a single reproducible result.

Rosh mixed work groups with both hard and soft practitioners, believing that they would find ways to work harmoniously on specific issues. But when they were placed in mixed groups, there were arguments and disagreements. They fought among themselves and they fought between themselves. Over time, their talents were compromised. The abilities of Ratzah to support its economic basis – namely knowledge – were squandered. Arguments broke out within experts in specific sciences and between experts of different sciences.

There were continuous arguments that were hard to hide from the planets they were serving. Arguments among themselves were viewed as a lack of knowledge and work concentration.

And as we found out in the past, the disagreements led to frustration and dismay by those most involved in these issues. These frustrations were not necessarily impacted on the workers themselves, but on Rosh, who supported the methods of mixed sciences in assignments. Since Rosh was in control of this policy, anger was focused on her.

Frustration in the past led to aggression – a universal law of behavior. It fell to the followers of the hard sciences to act on their frustration. An action group of hard scientists chosen from experts in mathematics, physics and chemistry was formed to change the policy of Rosh. But it was to no avail. Rosh indicated the policy of mixing sciences would be continued.

The leader of the mathematics function, **Calc,** reached the greatest level of frustration and decided to act on the need to reduce the exasperation. Calc asked to meet privately with Rosh to discuss the discontent of the mathematics group. Rosh continued to defend the policy further, frustrating Calc. Calc picked up a pointed tool that was used to represent trigonometry functions among mathematicians, and stabbed it in the organ needed to pump energy fluids in the body of the organism, bringing down Rosh. So upset with the action taken by him, Calc stabbed his own organ that pumped energy fluids, ending his own existence.

When the news of what had happened to the well-loved leader, Rosh, came to the community of scientists, they divided into groups of hard and soft sciences, and fought with each other. The war of the scientists lasted for over a year and thousands of the brightest minds were ended, as well as the economic foundation of Ratzah.

The leaders of the close-in universe attempted to develop a rule to prevent this behavior from happening again in the future.

Rule 6:

Do not murder another organism to satisfy your own frustration. There are classes of murder that may be accepted such as to save oneself from damage. But never act on your own frustrations to end the life of another organism.

CHAPTER
TWELVE

The War of the Stolen Partner

The experience of the Kokav-Zalzul War taught the planets of the close-in universe the importance of respecting and honoring one's parents. P'ari overthrew his father, Pr'am, to lead the Kokav planet, even though the people had chosen Pr'am as their ruler. It led to a harmful war with many organisms having their lives ended, including that of P'ari.

The developments of the rule of honoring and respecting a parent were the important outcomes of this war.

However, there is more to honoring and respecting a parent. Many organisms benefited by expanding the roles of the parent beyond honor and respect. The sages of the close-in universe recognized that there were many aspects of a parent's relationship with an offspring.

One of the major findings was that respect and honor lead to learning by example from the parent. The provider or birther sets an example for the offspring so that they will treat other organisms in a kind manner.

P'ari initiated the war by not considering the feelings and happiness of Mene, the ruler of Kokav. It was not that P'ari did not know Mene. Kokav and Zalzul had a major business relationship that worked to the benefit of both planets.

P'ari took Mene's birther, Hel'n as a prisoner. Originally, Mene offered to let Hel'n negotiate an agreement with P'ari to purify the gold. P'ari, having overthrown his father, Pr'am, rejected the years of learning that Pr'am had taught him about respecting the property and emotions of other organisms. He took Hel'n as an object of affection and reproduction. This act, as well as the killing and capturing of the hostages from Kokav, resulted in Mene attacking and starting warfare with Zalzul, causing many lives to end. It also sent those who depended upon P'ari into starvation and the end of their work and living standard.

The sages of the close-in universe met to develop a rule of behavior.

Rule 7:

You shall not take or attempt to divert the feelings and emotions of the partner of another organism – be it a birther partner, a provider partner, or a companion for whom great affection exists. Those that attempt these diversions will be punished greatly, for they endanger the order of the societies in which they live.

The War of Theft of Valuables

The Kokav-Zalzul war taught us another lesson. For many eras, Kokav provided Zalzul with great quantities of gold. Not only was the gold extremely valuable because the labor that Zalzul put into the gold was used by Kokav for space travel, but also to it was important to provide labor, sustenance, and housing to those on Zalzul.

P'ari, who had overthrown his father, had agreed to continue the task of carrying out the manufacturing requirements for processing the gold. As time passed, P'ari lost his ability to control his bad emotions. He felt that anything he wanted he could take: a father's kingdom; Hel'n, the wife of his trading partner, Mene; and the gold of Shamym. Our scientists believe that P'ari was withheld attention and love while growing up and felt that if he would not be given anything, he would take it.

We have already told the story of the war that emerged from the actions of P'ari, which led to a large number of deaths. The story of P'ari has been used to teach others that respect should be shown to a parent, and that you should respect the property of others, including their wives.

All of these bad actions in P'ari's life arose from his belief that he could simply take away what others own.

Our scholars explored these negative actions and prepared a Rule of behavior:

Rule 8:

You shall not take from another person or prime organism an object, either animate of inanimate, without the consent of the person or organism who owns it.

CHAPTER FOURTEEN

The War of the Dishonest Testimony

This tale is about one key planet in our close-in universe called **Tayvel.** It is approximately 9,000 miles in diameter and approximately 100,000,000 from their mother star. Very much like your planet, Aretz, it had many similarities that emerged from its form and development. Tayvel was a planet that had a provider/birther pairing that was permanent. A lifelong bond was formed by the pair in three phases: a way of finding and meeting the partner, a way of close courting the partner, and a way of culminating the courtship by providing a pledge in a ceremony for lifelong commitment. A trained spiritual leader did the final bonding.

Since the Prime-Organisms of the planet looked and emerged from the SWOW process much like the prime organisms of your planet, Aretz, there was a need for these spiritual leaders to carry out the ceremony for the lifelong commitment. Several thousand of these leaders were needed.

Their leaders contacted me, El Shadai, to teach and train these spiritual leaders. Since the rules of our close-in universe were complex, my task was time consuming. As there were many rules to be taught and understood, I created a title for these spiritual leaders. Using the language of my home planet, Kokav, I gave the title of each spiritual leader the name, **RAV,** which was the word in our language that meant **"Many."** Each spiritual leader was given permission to teach the many rules, interpret the rules, and provide spiritual guidance.

Since Tayvel was a planet that was open to freely selecting pairs of providers and birthers, it suffered from the possibility of the frustration chemical influencing satisfaction with their partner. Part of the teaching in which the RAV was involved included the process and control of the aggression chemical as a response to frustration. As El Shadai, it was my role to enable the most advanced bio-engineering of my experts to provide the directions of each provider/birther to allow them to make their spiritual pledge last a long time. The RAVs also were responsible for dealing with the entire family so that the offspring of the couple would not erupt into what the RAV called sibling rivalry.

It became clear that the role of the RAV would be extremely complex. The RAV became involved in the provider/birther interaction, yet both the provider and birther might have other provider/birther relationships. We have also seen that under some circumstances providers found support with other providers, because the pleasure associated with reproduction can be found with other providers. Birthers also found support and relationships with other birthers for the sake of the pleasure.

Many RAVs were overworked because, with the direct need for advice, the original pair of provider/birther had grown geometrically, so it was common for the RAV to be dealing with the spiritual needs of 30 pairs. The 30 pairs formed a group that they called a "congregation."

Imagine thousands of RAVs providing spiritual help to thousands of congregations. There were arguments within each congregation to get time with the RAV. There were fights between the members to be the first one to see the RAV. The RAVs were upset with the arguments and distrust, and many of them left the congregations to which they ministered.

Within and outside of the thousands of congregations, there were many angry prime organisms. Anger expressed itself in many ways, including by lying to the RAV so that he could not provide spiritual help. and tThis led to aggression. Since Tayvel was a technological planet, weapons that used laser cutting and magnetic force fields were available. It was not surprising that aggressive behavior happened between 4,500,000 primes in Tayvel, many of which resulted in end of lives. In my role as El Shadai, I called upon my Seraphim to develop a new rule.

Since the problem on Tayvel was set off by primes ignoring truthful testimony, the following rule was created:

Rule 9:

Do not bear false witness against your neighbor, your family, or your friend. Always speak truth and seek truth in your relationship with them.

CHAPTER
FIFTEEN

The War of Coveting and Desiring Goods that Others Own

The primes of Tayvel were a believing planet, and they honored the ninth rule requiring truth in the relationships between prime organisms.

Over the passage of several eras on Tayvel, the new behavior, based upon truthful relationships between extended families, impacted on the tasks that Tayvel provided to Shamym.

Tayvel's task was to deliver tools and weapons that would help me, El Shadai, the single leader of Shamym, to travel through the universe and reach planets in the solar system, in the close-in universe, and in the distant universe.

Their technology included laser weapons and tools, magnetic force fields, and psychological and sociological studies that were used to understand the organization and communicate with the organisms on the planets. Among these were language translators and digital translators, such as the system used for this document.

The scientists of Tayvel were brilliant designers, and in the course of designing certain weapons and tools, they were able to develop objects that were usable to people for their private use. For example, when spaceships from Tayvel entered the atmosphere of a planet they were approaching, they utilized a hovering function for the ship. It was based upon being able to scan and identify the mineral characteristics of the planet.

Once the characteristics of the minerals were analyzed in the mothership, the vessel was able to develop a negative version of the mineral characteristic, which had an opposing negative magnetic valence. Thus, a ship could float over the planet by simply using the natural magnetic equality point without using propulsion power. Similarly, the experts from Tayvel developed concentrated light sources called laser light. This technique was used for weapons if alien parties and organisms attacked our landing parties, and for surgeries to remove organs that might be injuring our torsos. Both of these used the ability of the concentrated light to cut through bodily organs without using standard weapons.

After the Tayvel population adopted the 9th rule, they no longer bore false witness against others on the planet. However, over several eras in time, Tayvel developed into a strong manufacturing planet. They used their technologies for developing and implementing their skills toward the challenges of creating devices that used the laser light and magnetic hovering weapons for the private use of their population. The concept was to make tools and "gadgets" for their citizens. The laser light technology, for example, was used to design and cut components of materials used in the dwellings in which they lived. The laser light technology was adapted to learning issues that are part of the education of the newly born Prime-Organisms. We found laser beams to be easier to read and, in some cases, could be used to improve the ability to see objects that were shown to young people.

After years of attempts, the hovering capability of the ships was used to develop a device connected to a prime organism's locomotion organs that permitted them to jump and hover. This was designed to provide gravity neutralizers – a smaller application of the larger one on their space ships. This approach was used as a means of individual locomotion. Young prime organisms transferred from schools to home and between divisions and subjects within school. The laser technology was found to be useful in drawing and describing new objects or products.

The design and manufacturing skills of the planet of Tayvel became prolific. They developed many functions that made their use of information, science, and transfer of knowledge.

It was not surprising that the development of personally owned and used objects led to prime organisms wanting to possess these objects for their own purpose. They had argued for a chance to buy or utilize one or many of these devices. There were minor skirmishes among those who wanted to have the opportunity to own these tools. However, these conflicts were not with other organisms. Rather it was for them to satisfy their needs of learning and using these objects. Coveting these objects went against the need for me, El Shadai, to have an orderly and peaceful population. The last law was developed to encourage good manners and peace within our society.

Our group of elders came up with a simple rule:

Rule 10: Do not go out of your way to become the owners of objects for your own pleasure at the expense of not sharing them with others. Coveting those objects at the expense of your family, friend, and neighbor is a selfish goal and does not work to the benefit of our society.

SIXTEEN

The Council Meeting of the Close-In Universe

After the 10 rules of conduct were introduce to the governors of the planets in the close-in solar system, all the planets in this solar system adopted these rules that had emerged from the wars. The leaders of Shamym called a council meeting with the leaders of the high intelligence planets. These planets were those that had developed earlier in their planet's life cycle and had a planetary environment that supported intelligence and science. This included the ability, by use of animal proteins, to grow larger functional thinking organs. Many of them had perfected the science of interplanetary travel and navigating the black holes in the universe.

These planets were concerned that the millions of Prime-Organisms that were lost in the 10 wars might have been a result of the development of intelligent life. Some of the scholars believed that the SWOW (Strong Win Over the Weak), while leading to the best characteristics for surviving in different environments, allowed for the development of weapons that could be used to exploit new sources of strength outside of the body. Their scientists had analyzed the wars and found that they were the result of two major factors in the universe.

The first factor was a lack of a standardized set of rules on how to behave amongst Prime-Organisms of their own species and Prime-Organisms of another species.

The second factor was the tendency of certain types and species of Prime-Organisms toward violent behavior, even if it leds to danger to oneself.

They were concerned that if these two factors were not controlled, there would be an endless round of wars and killing. Weakness was not a lesson learned by planets in other galaxies.

Accepting weakness as an outcome may require rules and regulations to recognize and even encourage weakness. However, if they do not learn our lessons and rules, they will be faced with death and insecurity, and even the end of their own close-in solar systems and civilizations.

As a result, the council decided that what their close-in universe had learned from these wars must be taught to other solar systems and planets in the universe. They sent out an exploration party, using the principles of interplanetary flight. These explorations tested new techniques of traveling through wormholes that enables their ships to exceed the speed of light and compress time. For several centuries of time they could identify many planets on which they could expect to find some form of life. They sent probes to the distant parts of the universe to identify planets that appeared to have life and were likely to benefit from the teachings and experiences of our close-in universe.

Before this major intergalactic trip, scientists in our solar system and close-in universe understood that we had to reach solar systems that were widespread in many other galaxies, solar systems, and universes. Chance was a great influence on finding these planets. Few of them were "lonely" planets, far away from other ones. Aretz, your planet, is a "lonely" planet and we decided that it was unlikely to be a planet open to the laws of our system. That is why the scientists of Aretz could never identify visitors over many eons of the history your planet, but legends of visits in the past became a common story.

"Stories of encounters with beings from other planets have been reported by many people from Aretz. The number of these encounters tend to come from humans within the past 100 years. It is likely that the science of Aretz is being reported to average humans and they are likely to imagine lights, sounds, and shapes in the sky as examples of visitors. There is even a reported area in the United States where evidence is said to be stored. Nobody has seen this evidence and there are more rumors about this than there are witnesses to seeing them. Few reports were made by humans over 100 years ago, probably because there was no knowledge about extraterrestrials. Some people believe that these visits from a long time ago might have occurred, but they may have been interpreted as a Supreme Being of some type."

Trips to these planets used the wormholes we identified many eons before. It was our explorers and scholars who recognized and formed the phenomena of wormholes.

Early studies found out that the waves of light within which we travelled were bent by the detritus of the particles that were moving away from the origin of the large explosion that started the universe. If we followed the light particles, the speed and time needed to go to faraway universes would be much longer because we would, by following the bent path of light, take more time following the light wave. In effect, we would be traveling a wavy path.

Since our scientists found that these wavy paths of light were folding over on themselves, they attempted to force paths of darkness through the bent light paths. It was difficult to do this, in effect, cutting a path of darkness through light paths. That is because the path would collapse. However, since we had mined large quantities of reflective gold for our travel through the universe, we were able use the reflection of light with the gold and in effect, interrupt the light paths with dark space holes. Previously we had described this process:

Shamym had the largest supply of gold in the universe. Our scientists developed a method of processing gold and changing it to a source of power. One way of deriving energy is by the power of the light of a mother sun. For many orbits of time, this ability was found to have high inefficiencies. It was not because the light was inadequate, but rather because most of the light coming to their energy sensors was not being absorbed.

They discovered that metals like gold, silver, and platinum had the ability to absorb the energy more efficiently by changing their surfaces to have millions of microscopic vertical cones so that the light entering it was completely absorbed. This enabled us to draw energy from even the most distant light sources to maintain trajectories and feed our heavy power needs when we were closer to a bright light source, such as a sun or even reflected from a nearby planet.

To enable the gold to absorb distant light, the Zalzul factories modified raw gold. It was made into flat continuous strips, and lasers cut beams of light, cone shaped channels. Zalzul provided these to Kokav and they were used for all of the power necessary for the functioning of the planet, its scientific research and development, and its travel to faraway worlds and galaxies. Most importantly, Kokav shared their abilities with Shamym and this became a key factor in the development of its science and travel.After we built these holes, we were able to use them to travel long distances to the areas of the universe we were exploring. Although our crews aged normally in our spaceships with compressed time, the ages of their family and organisms in their family increased at a faster rate than their age. The age differences were obvious when they returned to their planet and found their offspring older than they were.

The council approved a trip to examine the 400 planets and universes to explore whether the organisms of these planets had achieved a high enough level of civilization that we could consider safe to the planets in each of the close-in universes in their vicinity. The level of social development of these planets was peaceful and they had gone through a similar process of developing rules, as did our universe. We exchanged information on the process in which they had. After our visit to these universes, we asked them if they knew of other universes that had rules similar to theirs and ours.

They told us of a distant planet in a "lonely" planetary universe on the edge of their universe which they have been observing. It had recently exploded a nuclear bomb based upon the uranium fuel. The bomb had killed many. We were aware that since the bomb that was observed had exploded thousands of eons ago, we might be able to reverse the destruction if we could find wormholes that enabled us to reach these organisms in a short trip at a speed greater than light.

We built wormholes in 30 solar systems, one of which led to a path to Aretz, your planet. We could reach Aretz at a time that predated the nuclear explosion by approximately 40,000 Aretz years.

CHAPTER
SEVENTEEN

Observation of Aretz

When we arrived on Aretz we explored the planet. It had an atmosphere of 21 percent oxygen, 78 percent nitrogen, and 1 percent carbon dioxide and argon, similar to several other planets in our close-in universe. It consisted of two giant landmasses from pole to pole. Surrounding the landmasses were giant seas made up of bi-hydrous oxide.

Tests of the strata and substrata suggested that the great explosion that started the universe might have occurred 60,000,000,000 Aretz revolutions around its mother star ago. In that time the surface of Aretz was a mixture of hydrogen, oxygen, helium, and carbon.

Like our planet, Shamym, there was the process of survival of organisms previously discussed called SWOW – the strong win over the weak. This existed whereby those organisms that could survive the environment in which they were residing found new ways to advance their growth and functionality. Those that couldn't survive ceased living. So, life forms arose from the boiling liquid of chemicals, first expressing themselves as tiny particles, and then reproducing and growing within the liquid environment. Their first stage was as an organism that lived within a liquid environment, then some of them moved out of the liquid and survived on the lands. Many classes of sub-organisms existed. When we went into the atmosphere of Aretz, we observed large landmasses all surrounded by water. We saw that the Prime-Organisms of this landmass also had a tribal organization.

But they had not yet reached a stage of development whereby their knowledge was developed. Since large oceans surrounded this landmass, the sub-organisms of this landmass were different from those of the other landmasses on both sides of Aretz. Their uniqueness included ways of mobility by leaping large distances. We collected data on them and allowed them to continue using SWOW as a factor in their development.

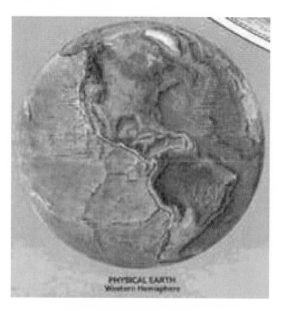

First Side of Aretz Observed and Classified:

Prime-Organisms of Aretz: The landmasses had several classes of prime organisms that differed from each other in their level of development and intelligence. Reproduction was accomplished in a pleasurable way with both providers and birthers living together as a pair for creating their offspring. Since pleasure was a use for reproduction, they were not behaving in a way that benefited the entire civilization.

The Upper Landmass: This upper landmass was made up of prime organisms that lived a simple life and fed their family groups with protein and amino acids by means of hunting and eating large sub-organisms in their area. Not unlike our societies, these prime organisms developed a society with a leader they called "Chief" who provided rules for living. These organisms lived happily within their environment but were not intelligent.

The Lower Landmass: The prime organisms residing in the lower landmass had similar rules of sharing, but a peaceful society was not always achieved. This was because the landmass was close to the equator of the planet and also had a range of mountains and eruptions due to release of hot liquids from the core of Aretz. As a result, there was a greater degree of competition for food, materials for shelter, and garments needed for the prime organisms. Several offspring of these tribal organisms formulated rules whereby visitors to the tribal areas were captured and sacrificed to the leaders they imagined they worshipped. They also were superstitious, murdering the firstborn child of a birther as a symbol of the entities they deified.

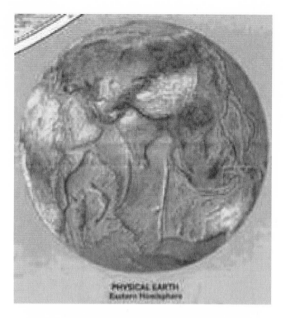

The Second Side of Aretz Observed and Classified:

The other side of Aretz also had three major landmasses.

Largest Uppermost Landmass: The largest and most populous was made up of prime organisms that had highly developed thinking organs. Because of the flat land in which they lived, which was close to the polar area which received less direct heat of their mother star, they were in a cold climate and their skin was of a yellow pallor.

Smaller Upper Landmass: Closer to the upper pole of the planet were pale skinned prime organisms living in cold climates. They hunted large organisms for protein and the fur that was attached to their bodies. Since the large organisms they fed on had evolved organs for self-defense – such as horns, sharp teeth, and speed of mobility – the prime organisms of the polar landmass developed strategies to survive using weapons that could be propelled over long distances with great accuracy.

Large Middle Landmass: A third land mass was extremely large and highly populated. It was situated close to the warmest equator of the planet, which was the area in which its mother star cast its most direct heat and light. Because of this constant heat, the landmass had many forests and jungles in which the climate had high levels of bi-hydrous oxide in the gaseous atmosphere of the planet. Within these forests, the prime organisms of the planet developed dark skin, via SWOW in all likelihood.

Over eons of time, these prime organisms evolved into the most capable to control the other sub-organisms, which likely enabled them to survive the heat and continuous energy of their mother star on their bodies. Our landing party descended to examine these Prime-Organisms closely. They lived in a tribal culture and hunted the sub–organisms. But we noticed that they were also hunted by the sub-organisms. In their culture there was much hardship. To deal with these, they developed a method of worshiping animals, many of which were geographic anomalies, and used the skins of these creatures as clothing to signified status within the tribe. These Prime-Organisms observed our landing party several times. They saw us as supernatural beings and it is possible that our landing became part of the history they wrote. But they knew nothing about our reasons for being there.

The Prime-Organisms of an Upper Middle Landmass: After observing and exploring these landmasses, we were ready to leave the planet. But our decision to do so was postponed by a discovery of another civilization. In between the uppermost and lowest landmasses, we found an area abutting on a large warm water sea, fed by rivers adjacent to loamy soil filled with nitrogen and surrounded with an atmosphere rich in oxygen and carbon dioxide. We decided to observe the prime organisms in this area and came to the conclusion that they had reached a level of intelligence that may have been the precursors of the Prime-Organisms who would be capable to explode a nuclear device in 5,000 years. Our observations were based upon what they had done in their environment.

Under the directions of a leader, **Adam**, they used the loamy soil that they found to grow food that was high in fibrous material and nutrients. They captured sub-organisms rather than killing them for food, then raised them, guided their reproduction, and used them to do various types of labor such as carrying and dragging heavy loads. In several species of sub-organisms, they used them to ride upon. They lived in peaceful woods with all types of trees providing edible fruits. Since we knew from our planets that the ability to grow thinking units was based upon the ability to consume a diet of amino acids and protein from lower organisms, we sent one of our leaders to them. He taught them which organisms they had captured would provide the proper diet for them to consume to advance their energy and muscle mass. Under their leader, **Adam,** this group classified these trees they had eaten their entire diet from as **"The Tree of Life."**

The foods we showed them that contained protein and amino acids increased their thinking organs. They referred to these foods as coming from **"The Tree of Knowledge."** Over time, they left the woods and built larger areas in which to live. Because of these advances in diets, they developed larger groupings of tribes and organizations. They traded with each other, offering sub-organisms of one type for sub-organisms of another type. We decided to extend our stay to follow their behavior at a distance.

Our scholars that helped us analyze the planet Aretz came to the following conclusions. The tribes of Avram had reached a high level of knowledge, impacted by the original visit we had when we interacted with their ancestor, Adam. Their knowledge of the foods from the land that they called the **Fruits of Life** provided vitamins and minerals for their strength and sustenance, and the use of the **Fruits of Knowledge,** to which we guided them, provided the amino acids and protein that developed their thinking organ. They became the most advanced of the tribes on Aretz, which enabled them to use knowledge and strength and survive on their landmass. Unlike other tribes, they developed a rudimentary series of rules to allow their strength and knowledge to be used for the benefit of their tribes.

As a result of a meteor colliding with Aretz, there was a major flood that occurred after 7,000 rotations around their mother star after they left the jungle in which we intervened. While other civilizations on Aretz lost many Prime-Organisms, under the direction of **No-a,** they had the knowledge to build a large floating craft to save the major families of their tribe. Samples of the lesser organisms were used for food and burdens.

CHAPTER EIGHTEEN

The Offspring of AVRAM

The group of prime organisms coming from the offspring of No-a adopted the food diet of both the "Fruits of Life" and "The Fruits of Knowledge." The leader Avram, who settled with them in another area, led the leading tribe. We approached Avram, believing that he would question who we were. It was common for the prime organisms now to shun and even fight with strangers that came over their land. Avram invited us into his habitant, offering us food and nutrition (although we did not partake in the food because our organs of sustenance would not be able to absorb the food.) Avram described us as "Angels," a word that depicts a perfect helper to a supreme leader. We were surprised with his accurate perception of who we were. It was clear that Avram had taught his tribe basic lessons of good behavior.

We followed the tribe through a period of over 800 years, during which the tribe grew. His sons, **Yitzhak** and **Yaakov,** took his place after he ceased to live and continued the rules of good behavior. One of Avram's 12 great-grandsons, **Yosef**, was asked for help by a neighboring group of prime organisms who were led by a leader they called **Paroh.** He came from generations of Pa-rohs who had much gold, wrote in a picture language, and were buried in giant vaults in multiple triangular shapes. Yosef, by teaching these Pa-rohs the importance of crop rotation, eliminated a major food shortage. He became one of the rulers of this society.

There were 12 tribes of Avram, who now numbered in the hundreds of thousands of prime organisms. They were invited by Yosef to settle in this new land. After 40 years, the size of Yosef's people were threatening to the Par-oh of this locale. They were like Yosef – intelligent, capable of designing tombs and buildings, and able to read and supervise others. The Par-ohs decided to capture and rule Avram's offspring and they became the forced workers under the Par-ohs.

We observed the tribes of Avram for many rotations around the mother star. The Pa-rohs treated the forced workers poorly. Some of the leaders wanted to keep the providers and birthers happy so that they could increase the number forced workers. They realized that to do this safely, they would have to limit the number of new providers so that the tribe of Avram would not be able to revolt against their leaders. They decided that the providers of the people who controlled the workers could mate with the birthers of the tribes of Avram. Over time, the organisms that came from those mating would be loyal to their Par-ohs. They ordered that all new provider (male) organisms born to the tribes of Avram be killed shortly after they were born.

The tribes of Avram gravely suffered over this rule. What birther would be willing to destroy their male organism? One birther hid her male organism in a floating box of reeds and hoped the tiny child would be saved. The offspring of the Paroh, who was a birther, found the young offspring of the tribes of Avram, and instructed him on the rules of the land. With our advanced science we were able to place the child at the time that the Par-oh was building the nation. Not knowing how to care for a child, she gave the child to his birther, her labor was caring for the child. As a result, the child was secretly raised as a tribe member of Avram. His name was Moshe.

Our observation craft followed the growth of this child and found that he was intelligent and strong. He also had sympathy for the tribes of Avram, even to the point of interfering with an overseer from Pa-roh who was punishing a worker from the tribes of Avram. He lived a life of a kind and sympathetic person. We communicated with Shamym and they agreed that we should use Moshe as a way of eliminating the hard work forced upon the tribe of Avram.

One day, Moshe was tending to a flock of animals whose fur was used to make clothing. We distracted him by placing a plant in his way that was burning but not being consumed. One of our crew-members projected his voice to the place of the burning plant. We asked him if he would lead the tribes of Avram away from the land of Par-oh. He said that freeing his tribes was his major desire. He asked the voice that was offering to help him, "Who are you?" Our crewmember answered Moshe, "I am who I am." This interaction had a major impact on the path the tribes of Aram soon took. It gave Moshe the strength and speech to convince Pa-roh.

Moshe approached the Paroh and asked him to let the tribes of Avram leave Egypt. Paroh realized that the economic foundation of Egypt was dependent on the free labor of the workers from the tribes of Avram. He refused to free them. Our ship had the subatomic bots that we had used against P'ari in one of the wars. These were the bots that could not be seen, but could aggregate into functional machines. Using the brain wave interception of thoughts, we were able to determine that there were no arguments or rewards that could convince Paroh to give up the workers. Our scholars recommended that if rewards could not influence Pa-roh, then he would have to be persuaded through punishment to him and those close to him.

Our landing crafts were much more sophisticated than the Pa-roh's scientists and wizards, who couldn't match them in their ability to impact the environment. We explored the lives of the people ruled by the Pa-roh and found that their environment was a mixture of agricultural needs as a source of food, raising protein rich animals, both water and land raised to sustain their growth. They were strongly connected to the Prime-Organisms that came from the paring of a couple. We also found that in the humid environment in which they thrived, they sought comfort from heat and attempted to prevent small organisms from feeding off their skin.

We suggested to Moshe that he should ask Pa-roh to free his workers. Pa-roh, who was not used to taking orders from organisms below his station, told Moshe he would not do it. Moshe told him that he would be punished if he didn't free them. Pa-roh laughed at him. "Who are you to tell me what I should do. As it is, I have fed your workers and allowed them to feed their own families." He chased Moshe out of his palace.

Moshe came to us crying and distraught. We told him that we might have to punish Paroh and his people. We thought the easiest punishment would be one that threatens the water source of Pa-roh. Since water alleviates thirst of prime and sub-Prime-Organisms, it would be the least damaging to Paroh.

On long trips our ships expended a large amount of ferrous oxide as a byproduct of propulsion. We sent many ships through the areas under the control of Paroh. These ships scattered the ferrous oxide in the streams feeding the large river that was the largest source of water for the nation governed by Pa-roh. The ferrous oxide turned the water red and gave it a ferrous taste. Pa-roh believed that the water had turned into blood. All organisms in Paroh's land stopped drinking the water. We allowed the ferrous oxide to disperse and Pa-roh believed that Moshe caused it. He told Pa-roh that his supreme being was responsible for it.

Still, Paroh told Moshe that he would not accept his entreaties, even after Moshe reminded him that he would be punished for not allowing his people's workers to leave the kingdom and be free of his control. But Pa-roh refused to even consider giving up the backbone of his economy.

Since it was clear that Paroh told Moshe that he would free the tribe of Avram, and then changed his mind after the plague, we used the changes to the water to impact the environment and create another plague. The change in the water quality enabled small insects called gnats to reproduce and bother the population by making their skin itch. Pa-roh did not keep his promise. The gnats were small and larger insects, called flies, came to eat them. Again Paroh ignored his promise.

We allowed many flies into the land. The flies were attracted to the dung and excretions of their cattle, and they blocked the breathing passages of their livestock's breathing tubes. Many of the livestock died and this caused a shortage of protein for the population. Again, Pa-roh reneged on his promise. The stench and dirt of the dead livestock filled the land and the people of Pa-roh broke out in skin sores full of eruptions. Again, Pa-roh refused to free the people of Moshe.

To clean the land and prevent too many animals from dying, our ship produced an area that made the rain freeze and large balls of ice fell on the people of Pa-roh. Pa-roh believed that the falling ice cleaned the land and therefore he refused to free Moshe's people.

While warned of other plagues, Pa-roh felt he had overcome the threats of Moshe. When the ice melted in the desert warmth and the trees began blooming, Pa-roh laughed at Moshe. But the blooming of the trees attracted locusts to feed of the leaves. The people of Pa-roh were bothered by the heavy darkness of the locusts blotting out the light of the mother sun, one of its deities. Some of the people began consuming the locusts but they were not happy about the darkness. It scared many of them. Moshe told Pa-roh that he would make the darkness permanent. Our large mother ship imposed its shadow over large areas of the land of Pa-roh. For several days there was no light and the people of Pa-roh were frightened.

Moshe again told Pa-roh that he would make a tenth plague that will be worse than any others. Pa-roh scoffed at Moshe, so we told Moshe to tell Pa-roh that even he and his family would be punished by the plague. Our ship had a supply of germs that were likely to make the young children of Paroh and his people sick and eventually dead. These germs were sprayed over the land of Paroh. The children of the tribe of Avram slept in rooms that had blood red markings in their homes. The markings contained antibiotics to prevent the germs from reaching them. All of the children of Paroh's people younger than 20 revolutions around the sun became ill and died.

Pa-roh and his court were full of sadness from mourning the loss of their children. Moshe reminded Pa-roh that he reneged from his promise and unless he freed his people, there may be another plague. In his sadness and mourning, Pa-roh told Moshe that he should take all of his people out of Egypt.

Moshe told his people that they should take their families, animals, and essential household items, pack them in their wagons, and head to the western edge of the desert toward the "sea of reeds." Moshe's people were a difficult group and complained, "Why did we leave Pa-roh's land to go into the desert? What can we do when we reach the sea of reeds?" When our landing party heard these complaints, we told Moshe that his people are stiff-necked!

Paroh had second thoughts about letting Moshe's people go free. He began chasing them so they could not leave Egypt. He hoped that he could capture his slaves and put them back to work. When Moshe's people reached the sea of reeds, they complained again because there appeared to be no way to cross the sea. Our large mother ship developed an idea that by firing a blast of heat at the sea, the water would turn to steam and enable Moshe's people to cross the sea at that point before the waters receded when the steam returned to the liquid stage.

The people of Moshe, the tribe of Avram, crossed the sea with their possessions. Then the armies of Pa-roh followed them into the sea to capture them. Sadly, when the steam condensed to the water state, the armies of Paroh were covered with the water and many of them died.

Moshe organized his 12 tribes of Avram, named by Avram's grandson, Jacob. They settled in the desert near the largest mountain. They were guided to the final land in which they would settle by one of our small anti-gravity ships. During the daytime, our ship's engine would be a smoky trail for them to follow, at night they would follow the flame of our propulsion unit.

The tribes of Avram complained often of the hardships they had to endure, despite the experience they had gone through from their escape from Egypt. Moshe decided that it was time for a new leadership to emerge in the tribes of Avram. Each of the tribes had a leader that represented them.

Moshe chose a new leader for each tribe and renamed the entire people after the new name that Avram's grandson, Jacob, adopted after he spent time arguing with me, El Shadai. He called me EL, which became an alternative name for me. When the two of us argued to reach an understanding, Jacob told me that he would like to change his name to ISRA-EL, meaning, "struggle with EL".

Moshe, to enable the new generation, changed the name of the twelve tribes from the "Tribes of Avram" to the "Children of Israel" which became the name of the nation that Moshe took charge of.

Our advance plan was to put this chosen group of organisms in an area that was verdant with plants and grazing land, and would provide space for each tribe. Our advance ship identified an area between a sea and a fresh water river. To reach it with the Children of Israel required a major trek through the desert. Moshe decided to use the leadership of the Children of Israel, organize the tribes, bring up and train a new generation, and conquer the land we had chosen for them.

Because of the large number of people that Moshe led, they had to travel a long distance to approach the new land. The Children of Israel needed places to camp and the ability to gather food in order to make the journey. Moshe estimated that it would take 40 revolutions around the mother sun for the Children of Israel to reach this new land. By that time, the new and younger leaders would be in charge of the people. Moshe's second in command, Yahushua (Joshua), would be the person to take over for him.

On the base of the mountain in the desert, Moshe addressed the multitude:

"Tribes of Avram, I will appoint over each tribe a new leader. We have found the land of Canaan which will be the home of our nation when we conquer it. It will take 40 years to reach that land. In that time, we will fulfill all the needs to live together. I will go up to this mountain to bring back a set of rules for us to live jointly as a nation."

Moshe climbed on the mountain in the desert of Sinai and met with me, El Shadai, on his ship that hovered above the mountain. It produced a loud noise that his tribes could hear on the bottom of the mountain. I told him that I would teach him 10 rules and that he should find a flat rock so that we can imbed the rules into the rock.

I shared with him each rule and discussed how and why they were developed. Moshe spoke to El Shadai, "The children of Israel, a stubborn group, needs more than rules. They have to be commanded to behave properly. *"When El Shadai asked me to express an opinion, I told him I agreed with Moshe. Command them to behave! Do not ask them to follow rules!"*

El Shadai agreed and Moshe wrote them down. Here are the rules, written on the stones.

First Commandment: *An Omnipotent leader acting in the interest of his people must be obeyed and respected. No activities or distraction that substitute for or lessen respect for the omnipotent leader shall be taken up. The people may practice activities and distractions but they must not be placed ahead of the leader and be used to reduce the importance or authority of the leader.*

Second Commandment: *If the Omnipotent leader is acting in the best interests of his subjects, it is forbidden to substitute a physical symbol of the leader as an image, nor shall there be a substitute in an abstract way. It should not be built, it shall not be used as a substitute for the leader and his demands and laws,- nor shall it be obeyed. Only the leader himself can create and rule on the commands, and if the command is made, the leader must be obeyed.*

Third Commandment: *You shall not take the belief of the omnipotent leader and His power in vain, for the leader will not hold guiltless those who take His name and existence in vain.*

The Leader stands alone Hear Oh Subjects! El Shadai is the only Leader from which all knowledge emanates.

Forth Commandment: *Enable a single day – the seventh day – as a Sabbath Day for rest and rejuvenation. Use it to learn new tasks and activities, relate to other organisms, and share the love of* *your environment and plan for the next week. Also use it to meet and enjoy the prime organisms in your family unit, and provide your thinking unit with a chance to recycle and learn.*

Fifth Commandment: *Show respect and honor to those who have birthed you and cared for you, your parents, for their experiences are better than yours for all of their lives. Do not overthrow them, harm them, or replace them unless they judge you to be their equal or superior.*

Sixth Commandment: *Do not murder another organism to satisfy your own frustration. There are classes of murder that may be accepted such as to save oneself from damage. But never act on your own frustrations to end the life of another organism.*

Seventh Commandment: *You shall not take or attempt to divert the feelings and emotions of the partner of another organism – be it a birther partner, a provider partner, or a companion for whom great affection exists. Those that attempt these diversions will be punished greatly for they danger the order of the societies in which they live.*

Eighth Commandment: *You shall not take from another person or prime organism an object, either animate of inanimate, without the assent of the person or organism that owns it.*

Ninth Commandment: *Do not bear false witness against your neighbor, your family, or your friend. Always speak truth and seek truth in your relationship with them.*

Tenth Commandment: *Do not go out of your way to become the owners of objects for your own pleasure at the expense of not sharing them to others. Coveting those objects at the expense of*

your family, friend, and neighbor is a selfish goal and does not work
to the benefit of our society.

Moshe brought the flat stone to us. Using laser weapons on
our ship, we cut the writings of these rules into the rock. Moshe's
brother Aaron was the spiritual leader of the tribe and he and Moshe
asked El Shadai if they could have a tabernacle to study the 10
Commandments in which they would learn and pray. Since our ship
had a large amount of gold, we built for the Children of Israel a large
area for praying and learning which could be carried from camp to
camp. Moshe carried the stones down to the Children of Israel and
started to teach and discuss them with his new, younger leaders in
the tabernacle. The tabernacle became the symbol of good behavior
and learning.

"I told both El Shadai and Moshe that I sense that the 40
years as a nation will turn the Children of Israel to a strong army
when it reaches Canaan."

El Shadai told me his discussion with Moshe, **"With Moshe**
not knowing the best way to get intoto Canaan, I told him that
we would guide the Children of Israel by asking them to follow
our hover ship. In the daytime, they could follow the vapor of our
rocket, at night the flame of the rocket. The 40 year trek was ardu-
ous, but each of the 10 tribes specialized in skills. The Children
of Israel became a strong force. In the desert, they fought the
Amalekite hoards that attacked the Children of Israel from the
rear, murdering many of the women and children of Israel. The
Israelite army sought revenge and conquered the Amalekite,
killing all of the army and seizing their cattle and food. They let
other nations know about their ferocious way of fighting and the

strength of their army. The other nations never again attacked the Children of Israel."

At the 38th year of the trek, Moshe died in old age having seen from a distance but not entering Canaan. The new leader he appointed was Yehoshua (Joshuah), who became the head of the army and commander of all of the 12 tribes.

The battle tested Children of Israel entered Canaan and conquered the Canaanites quickly. They divided the territory in to 12 states in which each tribe dwelled.

Yehoshua met with the 12 tribal leaders after spending time with Moshe before his death. Moshe was concerned that a major effort should be made to manage the functions of each tribe; growing and processing food, building homes, care for children and indolent members, resolving disagreements, building roads and water supplies, and other aspects of tribal operations, including organizing and training an army to defend the tribe.

Moshe and Yehoshua agreed that a second effort should be made to provide guidance and judgments on teaching and interpreting the 10- Commandments, and insuring that they became imbedded in the daily lives of the Children of Israel. Yehoshua chose Eliezer as the "Judge of Judges" to appoint 12 judges – one for each Tribe.

So, by decree, each tribe had a tribal leader and council to help run the functions of the tribe, and a tribal Judge to interpret the behaviors related to the 10 Commandments. There were also lower judges and magistrates to act to help the judge.

The organization of each tribe enabled equal attention to be given to managing the tribe by the head of the tribe, and to living a caring moral life by following the 10 Commandments, as taught by the judge of each tribe. Moshe had planned that all tribes be settled in the land of Canaan. But after Moshe died, two of the tribes (Gad and Reuben) were allowed to settle in the east side of Canaan across the Yardane (Jordan) River and in the heights of Golan.

The Tribes of Judah and Benjamin crossed the river and settled in the southern part of Canaan, while Asher, Dan, Ephraim, Issachar, Manasseh, Naphtali, Simeon, and Zevulun were the northern part of Canaan. The heads of the tribes were the best leaders chosen by Yehoshua. They are shown below. A special rule influenced the offspring of Simeon and Levi. Yehoshua did not make them head of a tribe, but Simeon was given the task of defending the Children of Israel, and Levi was given the job of being a ritual leader for all the tribes. Since the leader of the Children of Israel came from the tribe of Judah, Simeon merged with Judah and Benjamin after they reached Canaan.

In Canaan, the best leaders ruled the tribes. **Caleb** ruled Judah, **Shemuel** ruled Simeon, **Elidad** ruled Benjamin, **Bukki** ruled Dan, **Hanniel** ruled Manasseh, **Kemuel** ruled Ephraim, **Elizaphen** ruled Zevulun, **Paltiel** ruled Issascher, **Ahihud** ruled Asher, **Pedahel** ruled Naphtali, **Gershon** ruled Levi, and **Deuel** led the trib

The Development of the Children of Israel

After entering Canaan, portions of the land were given to each of the 12 tribes of Israel.

Once the tribes were in their places, our ship's communicators to Shamym decided to remove our ships from the area to allow the Children of Israel to settle in Canaan with little interference from us. They would guide their own destiny with their leaders and judges helping them in their decisions. Before we left Aretz, my appointed emissaries contacted the judges of each tribe. During the time that they settled in the land of Canaan, I wanted to make sure that in the action of settling and developing rules, the judges would be guided by the 10 Commandments of living. The judges were trained to keep the moral rules so that the daily rules of managing the details of tribal formation would succeed, guided by the 10 Commandments.

In the war, the southern tribes defeated the northern tribes and the Israelites separated into two kingdoms, Judah and Israel. The Kingdom of Judah was established when a Levi judge, Samuel, sought out a king of the Israelites. He identified a young man, Saul, who became the first king of Israel. While Saul was a good and beloved king, he was very insecure of his ability to rule. He was especially insecure about a young soldier in his army named David, who played a lute to enable Saul to have a calm sleep. But David was also a brave general and helped the Children of Israel conquer the Philistines by personally killing the head of their army, a strong and tall man named Goliath. Using a rock in a slingshot, he brought Goliath down and the Philistines were forced to surrender. Under the advice of Samuel, Saul put away his jealousy and permitted the kingdom to be transferred to King David.

David was a strong king of the Israelites. During his reign, the already existing city of Jerusalem became the national and spiritual capital of Judah. Yet David was an imperfect king. He fell in love with a beautiful woman, Bathsheba. When he found out that she was married to an officer in his army, he sent the officer to lead a battle and the man was killed in the fighting. David ordered that Bathsheba be brought to him and he took her as a wife. The judges and prophets that had followed the rules that El Shadai reminded the Children of Israel that by instituting the 10 Commandments, it was necessary to criticize David for coveting Bathsheba. As repentance for this action of going against the rule of coveting the wife of his officer, David spent many years of his life writing psalms to El Shadai looking for expiation. When David became old, his son, Solomon, inherited the kingship.

"In my study of the history of the Jewish people, I was often struck by the inability of bad behavior to be controlled by the leaders of the people. As we will see, King Solomon, one of the most

famous monarchs of the Israelites, was also known to misbehave. The king can't compromise his behavior. This would imply that the masses also had permission to misbehave. The prophets and judges did their best to warn the Children of Israel that they must follow the rules and commandments that created the Children of Israel."

Solomon, like his father David, had great capability which included building the first temple on Mount Moriah in Jerusalem, and writing poems to El Shadai when he was young (the Song of Songs), middle-aged (Proverbs) and old (Lamentations). Solomon expanded the kingdom by developing allies among other kingdoms. He often sealed these agreements by marrying the daughter of the king with whom he was negotiating. Solomon had hundreds of concubines. One important agreement spread the impact of Judah to the large continent south of Judah, ruled by the Queen of Sheba.

With the fracture of the Children of Israel, an Assyrian ruler, Tiglath-Pileser, conquered the northern kingdom of Israel 290 years after Solomon's death. There is no history about where the northern tribes were taken in battle. They are referred to as the 10 lost tribes. Our landing party was not able to find them. If we locate them in the future, we will communicate their whereabouts to the remaining Israelites.

The Assyrians were tolerant to the Children of Israel. They brought many of the Israelites to Babylonia and permitted them to continue their practices. Other Israelites stayed in Judah near their holy city of Jerusalem. A movement grew to interpret the entire Five Books of Moses (called the Torah) and the books of Joshua, Judges, Samuel, and Kings. In both Babylon and Jerusalem, different teams of rabbis poured over the Five Books and made the rules and regulations reachable to average Israelites. In many cases, the rabbis who prepared the Talmud softened some of the rules that were applied when the Israelites were a desert people. The Shamym landing party viewed these steps and occasionally, through communications and dream interference, impacted and advised the judges and prophets.

However, our choice of Canaan as a home to the Israelites resulted in unplanned occurrences. Because Canaan was situated between the northern land mass near the middle of the Eastern Hemisphere near a large sea, there were many large kingdoms to their north. South of Canaan and Philistine was the land of the Pharaohs and the large southern landmass. Since the armies of all these kingdoms warred with each other, the path they took for their wars ran right through Canaan. Approximately 225 orbits (years) after the Babylon exile, a new warlike king, Nebuchadnezzar, launched a war through Judah. To demonstrate his power, he destroyed the Temple of Solomon. His successor, Cyrus, found the Children of Israel to be excellent citizens of Babylon. He encouraged the Israelites of Babylon to return to Jerusalem and 70 years later, the temple in Jerusalem was consecrated.

During the next century, a major nation developed and became the strongest force in the Eastern Hemisphere. This nation was Greece. It was north of Judah and elected to spread its culture southward. Its culture was called Hellenism, a hedonistic way of living, concentrating on the human body and the perfection of the self. Greece had a panoply of gods representing aspects of living. Its culture ran counter to that of the Children of Israel that revered a single God, El Shadai, and his Commandments. 184 years after the temple was rebuilt, its leader and general, Alexander the Great, wanted to impact other nations with the Hellenistic way of life. His object was to take the Greek culture into Egypt, whose god was Ra, and to the Philistine people. He sent his troops through Gaza to Egypt. Because Canaan was a hilly country, he decided to bypass Judah and the Children of Israel. He attacked the two nations but sent emissaries to Judah and the Israelites to encourage them to adopt the Greek gods and teach them the Hellenistic culture. The Greeks took over the temple and encouraged Israelite scholars to translate the Books of Moses.

Many Israelites learned and accepted the Hellenist culture, but a group of religious Israelites revolted against the Greek teachings.

"In the story of the Greek conquest, I think of it as a parable for the 20th century, wherein time is devoted to the perfection of the body while charity, prayer, and help for the poor are ignored."

The Maccabees created a revolution and chased the Greek teachers away from the temple and rebuilt it. Ultimately, the Hellenistic empire was expelled and the Maccabee formed the Hasmoneans Dynasty which ruled the country. About a century later, another empire from the north attacked Judah and their center of belief, Jerusalem. Pompeii the Great lay siege to Jerusalem and the temple. To ensure that the Israelites would obey them, the Roman senate appointed Herod, himself an Israelite, to be the King of Judah. Judah and the Children of Israel were now under the control of the Roman Empire, governed by Israelite King Herod who was not even chosen by the Israelite judges and prophets. With the Temple as the center of prayer and sacrifices, the **Cohanim** (priests) that administered to the temple services and sacrifices also had no influence on the Roman control.

The next 60 years of the Judean kingdom resulted in major changes of the children of Israel. The Roman rule over the Children of Israel was harsh and the Romans sought a percentage of the donations given for the prayers and sacrifices of the temple. Since the Cohanim of the temple had to give the Romans a share of their donations, in order to maintain their living standards, they reported fewer donations to the Romans. The Romans, too, were not kind to the Israelites.

CHAPTER
TWENTY

The Schism of the Israelite Rabbis
and the Yeshuah Followers

The Romans noticed that strong beliefs, prayers, and practices provided a strong foundation of the Israelite religion. While the Roman society had many gods that they worshiped around their life and traditions, the Israelites had a strong belief in a single God – primarily my assistants and me. El Shadai, El, Adonai – all representing the word and my teachings. To overcome these beliefs, the Romans made it difficult for the Israelite teachers, prophets, and justices to assemble to pray and teach to their people. Well-known teachers, such as Hillel and Shamai, were forced to leave their congregations. In later years, Rabbi Akiva and his scholars were arrested and tortured. One rabbi, Yeshuah, who lived north of Jerusalem, and his followers were concerned about the way the priests were treating the temple in ways that made it difficult for the masses to share in the prayers and sacrifices of their temple. Yeshuah publically criticized the Romans for interfering with the Hebrews by forcing the priests of the temple to give them a tithe. He and his followers revolted and protested the roles of the priests by showing the Israelites that the priests were benefiting from those that offered prayers and sacrifices at the temple.

The Roman Emperor Pompeii and his local leader, Herod, were not happy with the insurrection of the Yeshuah Hebrews. They ordered troops to arrest Yeshuah and put him on trial. He was found guilty, and Pompeii had him executed by the Roman penalty of crucifixion. Many Israelites were followers of Yeshuah and his teachings. His parables, his ethics, his examples, and his goodness were admired by many Israelites for whom he was an activist rabbi. Many of his beliefs were grounded by the 10 Commandments, the rules of the Torah, and many of the rules developed by the rabbis in Babylon and Jerusalem in the Talmud interpreting the Torah. His followers believed that he was the Messiah who came from the line of David, the King. They organized their sect and lived in Judah and while they diverged from other Israelites, they followed their ancient beliefs.

The remaining Israelites sought new ways of prayer and learning. About 70 years after Yeshuah's death, the non-Yeshuah Israelites continued to fight the Romans and chose a mountain, Masada, which overlooked the Dead Sea, to have a last stand against the Roman army. Overwhelmed by the Roman siege, the population of Masada – every man, woman and child – committed suicide rather than be murdered by the Roman legions. To completely end the revolution, the Romans destroyed the second Temple in Jerusalem. These Israelites who had not accepted Yeshuah stayed close to their rabbis. The reasons for their non-acceptance of Yeshuah lie in several of the 10 Commandments, which were strict by not having a figure that competed with El Shadai.

Some of the leading rabbis were followed 90 years after Yeshuah's death: Shimon ben Gamliel, Yochanan ben Zakai, Yehuda ben Baba, Joshua ben Hannania, Eliezer ben Hercanus, Rabbi Gamliel and Eleazar ben Arach.

About 131 years after Yeshuah's death, the Roman Senate appointed Hadrian as Emperor of the Israelites. His first edict was to outlaw circumcision (one of the major customs of the Israelites that began with Abraham.) The practice of circumcision was strongly imbedded in the rabbis and Israelites who did not accept Yeshuah. A group of warriors led an insurrection headed by a leader, Bar Kochba. Hadrian punished the revolutionaries and to set an example, killed almost the entire population of the Hebrews – over one half million. Hadrian also destroyed the temple in Jerusalem. Many of the great rabbis were martyred – Akiva, Tarphon, Ishmael, Eleazer, Yose, and Elisha (a rabbi but an Apostate). New generations of rabbis began meeting and praying with groups of Israelites with poems and songs to God, but without animal sacrifices. The Israelites lived within the Roman empire and Judah was named Syria Palaestina. Many of the Israelites lived in hiding, but when Hadrian died, the persecution of the Israelites was stopped, an economic benefit to Rome and the Center of the Israelites.

The Yeshuah followers had success in converting the Romans to the Yeshuah religion. To make conversion acceptable, they were willing to change several traditions. Circumcision was made optional and the Israelite Torah was considered "old" and mostly replaced by a "new" book written in Greek, recounting the story of Yeshuah and his followers.

At about the same time this happened, the rabbis of the Israelites develop the Talmud that further united the Israelites. The Yeshuah followers were called the Christians, and the head of this group became the Roman Emperor Constantine. About 300 years after Yeshuah died, Constantine, feeling that the Christian religion should rule as head of the empire, enacted laws that were restrictive to the Israelites. Conversion of Christians to Israelites was outlawed and congregations for religious services were curtailed, but Jews were allowed in Jerusalem for the anniversary of the destruction of the temple.

Constantine sent his mother, Helena, to Jerusalem to obtain objects that could be traced back to Yeshuah. She found several objects in one of the many stores that collect these holy items, including a shroud that could have been used by Yeshuah after the crucifixion, and a part of a wood cross on which it was thought Yeshuah was tortured. When she returned to her son, Constantine, he used the image of the cross with Yeshuah on it and the shroud as symbols of the origin of Christianity. These symbols were used to drown out the Israelite religion. The concept of supersession, the new overcoming the old, resulted in the Israelites of Judah being called the "Judahs" by some and "Jews" by others. It gave Constantine the right for the Christians to punish and even kill the Jews in the name of their religion. Constantine and others destroyed many Jewish communities and homes.

"As we monitored the Israelites, I suggested to El Shadai the similarity with the Bagida experience. El Shadai became upset

because what happened with Constantine was very like the war in Bagida. A new set of rules overthrowing and killing the followers of the old rule for power."

El Shadai, angry with Constantine, positioned the spacecraft to create punishment. He aimed a vibratory force at the Galilee that shook the earth and decimated many of the Romans and some Israelites under Constantine's rule. Years later, the Empress of the Romans permitted the Jews to return to Canaan. This was followed by the Israelites combining the Babylonian Talmud and the Jerusalem Talmud to encourage the rules the Jews would follow.

Over time, the ship meted punishments to those people that did not act properly and ignored the 10 Commandments. Population centers were damaged and sources of food and water were minimized as an example to those who were not acting in a moral way. El Shadai made it be known by demonstration that bad behavior would not be tolerated.

"With my knowledge of history, I told El Shadai that he should be slow to punish the Christians simply because he was known as a God who had pity and did not anger easily."

This era became known to the world as the Dark Ages. The scouting party rewarded kindness and knowledge, and punished selfishness and stupid behavior. The Israelites, by dint of their Talmud, were free of these punishments by El Shadai, but not free from the oppression of the non-Israelites.

When they returned to explore the impact of the great experiment of punishing the enemies of Israelites, they observed dark ages 802 to 1,000 years after Yeshuah. They observed how the Jews were changed, ruled over by the descendants of the Roman and Israelite Christians. They found that the Jews still followed the Torah and basic principles of the 10 Commandments. The entire books of the Torah and the Talmud were made secondary to the Yeshuah followers of the churches of Christianity and the immovable beliefs of Islam, an Aramaic offshoot of the Jews and Christians.

Perhaps the lesson to be learned was that by accepting a single superior belief system of the 10-Commandments, the infuriated Christians and Islamists made the Jews secondary to their rules of the church and mosques, and the Jews came to represent a false God. Major battles were fought between different Christian offshoots and the offshoots of the Islamic faith, and the Jews were often punished and blamed in these battles. El Shadai and my visiting party found that they could not control these battles, even with the superior strength of their hidden spaceship. They came to believe that one party couldn't change the way people think, despite having a lot of experience in the proper ways of relating to the people in your society.

"Before they left Aretz, El Shadai and his teachers and judges left me in Jerusalem and their ship took them to other parts of the planet. They went to an area that had the highest mountains and a people led by a kind and good leader named Buddha. While the people of Buddha accepted the principles of the 10 Commandments, Buddha modified them but taught their meaning to his gentle people. He also reached some of the tribes on the other side of Aretz. They accepted their meaning but did not use them as a serious belief system."

El Shadai and his crew left the solar system of Aretz and visited other systems that had not been exposed to the 10 Commandments. They were getting ready for a major trip to Aretz to avert the nuclear event they witnessed many eons ago.

"Before leaving, El Shadai called to me. He said that I should be prepared to return to the ship to move forward in time to the year 1930 since the death of Yeshuah, the way the calendar was calculated. El Shadai told me "We are going into the future and we will need your knowledge of the history of your age."

Our ship set a course from a path to several solar systems that were 15 light years away from Aretz. The travel was using an approach wherein we moved through worm holes at an average speed of eight light years for the trip. We also taught the five solar systems the 10 Commandments, of which they memorized and learned together with our teachers and judges from Shamym. They provided this knowledge to the leaders of these planets and taught them the rationale for these teachings.

"I witnessed this process and I can tell you that none of the five solar systems had anything like slavery and plagues. They were peaceful populations, had apparently met and interacted with Shamym, and were ready to accept these moral advances for their population."

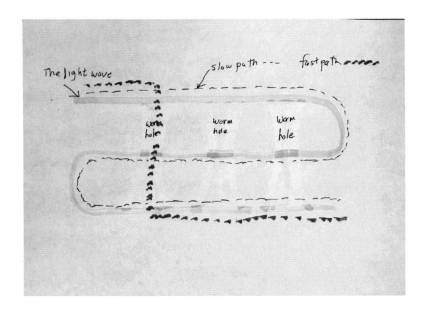

CHAPTER
TWENTY-ONE

The Return to Earth

The next stage of our trip was a return to Earth. This trip was going to reach a speed that was faster than light. To accomplish this, the ship rode the light beams in space at the speed of light. Since the light would be wavy, the time to reach Earth would be slower than the speed of light. To increase the speed, we created several worm holes made of the gold rods created for Shamym to absorb the light. By entering and exiting the worm holes, the ship jumped forward in time.

The ship arrived on Earth in a hidden orbit at the edge of the moon. At this stage of the trip, El Shadai asked his traveler to provide information.

His first question was, **"Can you judge whether our ship could be seen by the Humans of Earth?"**

"My guess is that it is likely that the spaceship will not be seen from this vantage point. Although there were telescopes pointed

into the sky, they were primarily used to explore the suns and planets in the sky."

Since El Shadai was truly concerned about the Children of Israel who he had freed from bondage, he repeated, **"Can we visit or observe the Children of Israel?"**

I provided a history lesson to him of the Children of Israel, *"Let me explain their history to this age. When we left Aretz to navigate back to Earth, it was the sixth Century (from the birth of Yeshuah). Many Hebrews were still in the land of Canaan. They were being punished by the followers of Mohammed, who were called the children of Islam. In the seventh and eighth Century, many of the Hebrews settled in the southern part of the northern landmass which was, and still is called, Europe.) They settled in such nations as Spain, Portugal, France and Italy. As guests in these nations, they were often victimized – sometimes by the Christian population and sometimes by the Islamic population. Since they moved freely between these nations, they became involved with trade and bartering. That was because many of the Hebrews were living in different nations without monetary standards. Thus, the Hebrews trusted other Hebrews for credits and loans. As a result, Hebrews became important to financial trading and they were important to the bartering of the nations within which they lived.*

I continued, *"Not all of them were traders. Many of them studied the Torah and Talmud, and the rules that emerged from the 10-Commandments were interpreted as new books were written, some for laws of behavior, some for mystical theories of life – Like the Kabbalah---and some written for prayers to you."*

El Shadai's next question was a repeat of the last. "**Can we visit or observe the Children of Israel?**"

My answer included an historical overview of the Children of Israel, *"The 10ᵗʰ century was a good one for the Hebrews. They found ways of living peacefully with the Islamic rulers of Spain. Both Islamic and Hebrew humans shared one God – The Hebrews called him El and Islamic humans called him Allah. It was called the "Golden Age." However, for the next two centuries, the Islamic rule weakened and Christians wanted Hebrews to convert to the followers of Jesus and give up their Hebrew beliefs."*

"Some of the Hebrews moved into the Norman countries, Britain and France. Many who refused to convert were killed or expelled. Hebrews moved to lands close to the Mediterranean (such as Iraq, Italy, Northern Africa) or into Western Europe where they could farm and build under a feudal system. Since the Hebrew people were spread out, the rabbis tried to codify the laws and traditions of the Hebrews. Some of the Christian Popes were kind to the Hebrews, but local groups of uneducated Christians often killed the Hebrews. So, to answer your question, we must look in the European nations, the area of the Mediterranean Sea, and the land of Canaan and its surrounding nations. I will tell you that in the next 10 years, an evil despot from Germany will murder many of the Hebrews."

El Shadai asked, "**Are there any ways in which we could prevent this from happening?**

After some time for thought I answered, *"No, I can't because I am but a human and only you can avert the decree. But if you acted, it might impact the future. Changing history could change the future. which would not have happened if you changed history. If you wish to have an impact, you should consider punishing those evil humans and helping the victims that could escape to find a way to survive.*

Think of the past, *"When you guided the Children of Israel in the desert, the Egyptians and Amalekites killed many Hebrews, but the result was that the remaining Hebrews crossed the Red Sea of Reeds safely reaching Canaan.*

Many people I knew when I was on Earth survived the Nazi period and went on to provide great benefits in science, medicine, art, and politics. Many of the survivors rebuilt the Land of Canaan, and named it Israel commemorating Yaakov's wrestling with you."

El Shadai said to me, **"You remind me of your grandfather. Rather than changing the world for a reason I am angry about, I am not willing to imagine how my anger might impact others'. Your solution considers other's lives. It is a difficult position to take. I am sure that in the future when the Children of Israel discuss the evil people of Germany killing the Hebrews, some will ask 'How could El Shadai let this happen?'"**

I reassured El Shadai, *"Yes, some will not survive, but they will still revere you for the positive things you give them: life, love, the birth and the growth of new humans. Over time, your Children will acknowledge you in prayer as being merciful, gracious, endlessly patient, loving, true, showing mercy to thousands, forgiving iniquity, transgression and sin, and granting pardon."*

El Shadai viewed the evil inflicted on the Hebrews by the German. He watched as they destroyed the homes of the Jews, beat and killed many families, stole their possessions, sent them to camps and starved them, and in the end, killed the Jews using mass killing machines. Millions of the population of Jews were murdered and families were destroyed. El Shadai, despite his promise to be calm, had anger, but he promised he would express his anger calmly.

I had to assuage his sorrow, *"I see your anger. Rrather than punishing the Germans you should reward the Jews. There is a Jewish Scientist, Albert Einstein, who has a knowledge that was almost as great as yours. I remembered reading when I was young, that Einstein could free the Jewish scientists from Europe to England and the United States. That move helped the Allies and prevented the Germans from inventing atomic weapons."*

"I suggested that just as you came into my dreams, you might be able to enter Einstein's dreams to help free many Jewish scientists and fulfill the history I read about in my youth."

Several Earth days later, he reached Einstein. Einstein asked him if he could reach a large group of scientists which he couldn't do by himself without alerting the Germans. He gave him a list to reach. Again, the ability of El Shadai to appear in human dreams was a unique power dating back to Adam, Noah, and Abraham (and Annie and me too!)

Let Einstein give him a list of how to reach them by title and status. El Shadai suggested that they gather in the city of Bayeux in Northern France. Einstein arranged a boat to England. El Shadai promised that Bayeux would be protected by his ships. When he saw a list of Nobel Prize winners, he was reminded of my description of Nobel and he was impressed. In the list of scientists that were

Knights, He didn't know what "Sir" meant. I suggested it is "angel" to a king.)"

EINSTEIN'S LIST

- **Nobel prize winners**: Prof H A Bethe, Prof M Born, Sir Ernst Chain, Prof M Delbruck, Prof D Gabor, Dr G Herzberg, Prof J Heyrovsky, Sir Bernard Katz, Sir Hans Krebs, Dr F Lipmann, Prof O Loewi, Prof S Luria, Prof S Ochoa, Dr M Perutz, Prof J Polanyi, Prof E Segre.

- **Knighthoods**: Sir Walter Bodmer, Sir John Burgh, Sir Ernst Chain, Sir Hermann Bondi, Sir Geoffrey Elton, Sir Ernest Gombrich, Sir Ludwig Guttman, Sir Peter Hirsch, Sir Otto Kahn-Freund, Sir Bernard Katz, Sir Hans Kornberg, Sir Hans Krebs, Sir Claus Moser, Sir Rudolf Peierls, Sir Nikolaus Pevsner, Sir Karl Popper, Sir Francis Simon.

All of them were awakened last night and transferred to Bayeux.

El Shadai placed the ship is a different hidden orbit. The crew observed the European war, the bombings of London, the broadcasts of Hitler's hatred. Several times El Shadai caused an "accident" to punish the German armies. Using a laser on his ship, it was possible for arms depots to be exploded when the laser beam was aimed at the ammunition and weapons storage areas. To the Germans, these explosions were thought to be sabotage from local resistance groups or malfunction of the storage methods.

The ship's crew also saw bombings coming from armies from the east and west. The crew members were curious as who these armies were.

El Shadai asked me, **"Can you tell us who are the armies coming from the west over the large sea?"**

My explanation, *"When your ship first came to Earth to explore from a distance, there were two large land masses on the opposite side of Earth, west of Europe across a large sea which we call the Atlantic Ocean.*

This is the nation from which I came. After thousands of years during which there were local tribes living on the northern land mass, many humans settled in this land, coming from the European nations across the fertile crescent of the warm water sea."

"The major reason that they came was because there were religious feuds, mostly between different Christian sects, and between Christian sects and Jewish sects. Many of the humans that came from the eastern half sought an end to these feuds. These people were followers of the 10- Commandments, and they believed in tolerating people of any sect. Various Christian groups sailed over a large sea, and Jewish people came because of the difficult life in the nations of Spain, Portugal, Germany, Russia, France, and other smaller Christian ruled nations."

My home nation was founded on what was called Judeo-Christian beliefs which used the rules of peace, love, and tolerance. For over 300 years, my country, called The United States of America, has lived together and created the rules of government that respected Judeo-Christian prayer and rules, which meant the decision of how you pray is not dictated to you. The rule of my country was to allow any human to practice his or her belief system and not insist that one faith or God must rule over another."

El Shadai asked me another question, **"With you updating me, tell me about who the attackers from the East were?"**

My answer to him was *"East of Germany were nations that included Russia and its satellite allies, and Asian nations including China and India. One of the strongest nations to its East was Japan, which joined Germany against The United States of America in 1941 by attacking a string of United States Islands called Hawaii."*

For several years, the spacecraft viewed the end of the war. The German nation was left in rubble. The head of the nation, Adolph Hitler, went into an underground bunker and ended his life. The armies and navies of Germany surrendered. The crew of El Shadai were expecting that Germany or Japan, as a last opportunity, would use the nuclear bomb that we saw many years ago. When it exploded, El Shadai did not know who set it off, nor what the damage was.

I explained the answer, *"The bomb was invented and used by my nation, The United States of America. The design and use of the bomb was created by many scientists that were freed from Germany by El Shadai. In the United States, they could conduct atomic research. The bomb was developed by Albert Einstein and his group. The leader of the United States, Harry S. Truman, carefully chose to use the bomb for the following reasons:"*

"In the war against Japan, the soldiers of the United States fought Japan in a string of islands off the Japanese coast. In one battle, to capture the island of Iwo Jima, the United States lost more than 25,000 marines. On another Island, Okinawa, the United States lost about 60,000 marines and the Japanese lost many more soldiers.

At the end of the war, the United States offered Japan terms of surrender, which Japan refused. The only way to convince Japan to surrender would have been by capturing the Island of Japan. President Truman estimated that to capture the home island, the United States would lose over 100,000 marines. Many hundreds of thousands of Japanese would die as well.

So, President Truman decided to use the atomic bomb on two cities in Japan which killed 129,000 Japanese citizens and no Americans. The Japanese surrendered immediately and ended the war."

El Shadai reached back into his memory to understand my comments. **"Your President Truman made a good decision. He obeyed this Commandment."** He pulled it out of the scrolls and said: **"Look at the Commandment."**

It read:

"Sixth Commandment: *Do not murder another organism to satisfy your own frustration. There are classes of murder that may be accepted such as to save oneself from injury or death. But never act on your own frustrations to end the life of another person.*

Under the control of El Shadai, the ship from Shamym moved into an orbit on the far side of the moon. They used this time to refuel and draw minerals from the moon that would help propel the craft back to Shamym.

El Shadai spent time with his visitor to discuss how the lessons of the Scrolls could be used for the benefits of the humans on Earth. His visitor quickly wrote down what he said.

"For many civilizations, the rules that leaders have created came with the belief that there is an invisible omnipotent God and you must do his will and obey him."

"However, this belief required people to imagine a Supreme Being, a God, with which they have no personal attachment, nor have spoken to him or seen him, and are afraid of how they will treated by him."

"So, in many civilizations, there are groups of people that have to imagine what God wants. Some of them kill people they do not like or are different from them because they say it is 'God's Will!' (As if I have a will to kill.) They attack and kill children because their adults have a different image of their God or don't accept their concept of God. And most important, they believe that God wants humans to behave a certain way. They build laws that are not like the 10- Commandments, such as dictating with whom you can live, and how many organisms you can produce. They believe that others reject God, and therefore they do not act in a moral way. Some say during times of upset, 'God is Dead!' They lose the optimism of living."

He finished by saying, "**I AM NOT THAT TYPE OF GOD!!**

"El Shadai wants his Prime-Organisms and Humans to be satisfied when they follow the 10-Commandments because it is the right thing to do. These commandments prevent wars and increase goodness and love to Primes and Humans."

"The Scrolls that I left in Shiloh describe a God who has seen real Prime-Organism and human behavior, both positive and negative, and draws rules and lessons that humans and organisms of all types can obey to improve their world."

"But it is not because the God says so and he will make your life better. Rather, the rules and laws are yours to see and understand, because the God concept came from Shamym. God met humans on Earth and influenced Prime-Organisms on many worlds. He has told you why these 10 rules (or Commandments) must be followed. It is that simple and it is up to you to pass on and follow why we wrote these Commandments."

AFTERWORD

The spaceship moved quickly over Shiloh, preventing its image from being seen by the defense systems of the modern Children of Israel.

While hovering over the tent in Shiloh, they used the small hovering ship to send me down to the area and the tent I had put up. I was surprised that it was still there as I had set it up. ago. I found the marble box of scrolls on the table, still wrapped in my Penn State windbreaker. El Shadai sent them down with me. I noticed that attached to the marble box was a list of the preeminent bible scholars, Rabbis, Priests, Ministers and Imams. It is up to me to tell God's story to them."

El Shadai had left me a note. **"Tonight, these scholars will have a vivid dream. Many of them will be in touch with you. You have much work to do and minds to change and to teach."**

"I took my cell phone out of the pocket of the windbreaker to call my nephew and asked him if he could pick me up where he left me in Shiloh.

Shmuel, my nephew, was happy to hear my voice: "I hope you were fine last night after we left. You must be tired, I'll be there soon, Uncle. Did you have a good night's sleep?" Ahh the pleasures of Time travel.

The End of The Beginning